# Girl in the Attic

# Girl in the Attic

VALERIE MENDES

SIMON &
SCHUSTER

*My deepest gratitude goes to Stephen Cole for his*
*enthusiasm, encouragement and brilliant editorial eye*

SIMON &
SCHUSTER

First published in Great Britain by Simon & Schuster UK Ltd, 2002
A Viacom company

Simon & Schuster UK Ltd
Africa House, 64-78 Kingsway, London WC2B 6AH

A CIP catalogue record for this book is available from the British Library

ISBN 0 689 83680 5

3 5 7 9 10 8 6 4 2

Printed and bound in Great Britain by Bookmarque Ltd, Croydon, Surrey

*For Sam*

Nathan didn't see it coming.

On that last day of the summer holidays he sat at Tom's desk, his sketchbook on his knees, as if it were an ordinary morning. Tom, wedged into his beanbag, engrossed in *Lord of the Flies*, was today a still and willing subject.

Nathan's hair stood up in spiky black strands as his charcoal lovingly skimmed and scraped the paper's surface. And snapped.

Nathan cursed. "That's messed up your chin. And it's my last piece."

"You shouldn't press so heavily." Tom read on.

"I don't. It's artistic fervour ... It's almost finished anyway." Nathan stood up, stretched his back and arms. "Let's go for a swim. While we still have our freedom."

"You'd better fetch your things, then." Tom glanced at him. "And get some more charcoal from your desk while you're about it. You never finish anything properly."

"Yes, I do."

"No, you don't. You check that book of sketches and tell me how many need more work."

Nathan threw a pillow at Tom's head and clattered down

the stairs. He and Tom lived on opposite sides of the same south London square. They'd met when they were six and had been best friends now for more than seven years. As they grew, they looked less alike: Nathan tall, gangling, dark-haired; Tom neat, small-boned, freckled. Nathan scatterbrained but sometimes brilliant; Tom methodical, thorough, organised as an army of ants.

Nathan Fielding and Tom Banks. Weed and Banksie. Closer than two fingers on a hand.

Now Nathan began to run across the square. Then he stopped. His trainers squealed like mice. The front door of his house gaped open. Bags littered the steps and Dad's Ford stood outside. But he'd left for work that morning. Why was he home? Perhaps he had to go on a business trip. He hadn't said anything, which was odd.

Dad came to the door, his grey hair falling over his forehead. Then Mum burst out on to the step. She tried to stroke Dad's shoulders, as if she were pleading with him. But Dad shrugged her off and picked up the bags.

Cold slivers stabbed at Nathan's throat. "Dad!"

Dad hadn't heard him. He ran down the steps and flung the bags into the boot. He climbed into the car, revved the engine and swung out of the square. Mum stared after him. Then she turned and slammed the door.

Nathan raced into the house and made straight for the kitchen. Mum had lit a cigarette. Her face shone with sweat and her straight dark fringe lay damp on her forehead.

"I've just seen Dad leaving." Nathan's mouth tasted sour. "What's going on?"

So Mum told him. That Dad had left them to live with a girl called Karen. She was a designer on Dad's new music magazine. Karen was divorced. Karen had a three-year-old daughter. She lived near Primrose Hill. Dad had been in love with her for ages.

Disbelief buzzed in Nathan's head like a trapped wasp.

"It's absurd." Mum crushed out the cigarette. "I spend my life as the nation's agony aunt. Tell me your problem and 'Dear Lizzie' can help. But when it happens to me, all I want to do is curl up in a dark room and cry."

Blood rushed to Nathan's face. *Dad with another woman.* "I don't believe it."

"It's the truth, so you'll have to." She reached across the table to grip his hand. "I know it's a shock, but you'll see him lots. That's what he wants." Her fingers tightened. "He loves you very much."

"What a great way to show it." Nathan wrenched his

hand away. "He's dumped me like I don't even exist."

"I'm not defending him." Mum looked suddenly older, crumpled. "But I don't want you to take *against* him ... He's coming to lunch on Sunday."

"But this is Monday. School starts tomorrow. I can't start a new term without Dad."

"You'll have to. He needs time to settle in with Karen."

"So where's his time for *me*? He'll always be somewhere else, on the end of a stupid phone."

"I'll leave you alone to talk on Sunday. I won't get in the way of you and Dad. I promise. I'll make sure you stay in touch."

"This morning," Nathan said, remembering how he and Dad had made breakfast together. "You must've been pretending like mad."

"I wasn't pretending. I hoped he'd change his mind. Just now – I prayed he wouldn't drive away ... Do you think I *wanted* this to happen?" She stood up and held out her arms. "Come and give me a hug."

Nathan glared at her. *I don't want you. I want Dad.* He threw back his chair, ran from the kitchen up to his room, slammed the door. He stared at the crumpled duvet, the untidy desk, the scattered books and comics. His head throbbed.

Mum tapped on the door. "Nathan? Are you OK?"

"Yes." *I must not cry.*

"I'm late for a meeting –"

"Don't worry about me. I'm going back to Tom's."

"See you tonight, then. I'll make us something special."

"Whatever." *Leave me alone.*

He leaned against the door, listening. Feet ran down the stairs and the front door slammed. He went to the window. She looked back at him but neither of them waved. Then she walked on.

For a moment Nathan wanted to run after her, to tell her everything would be OK. But anger returned, squashing the pity. He ran downstairs and out to the steps. The air stank of fumes. Another car was parked where Dad's had been.

Needle tears pricked his eyes. He walked, the square a blur.

Tom stood by his front door. "So where's your swimming gear?"

Nathan stared at him. "What?"

"Wake up, Weed. You look as if –" Tom's eyes narrowed. He moved down the path towards Nathan. "Something's happened."

"You could say that." Nathan gripped Tom's gate. "It's my dad."

Nathan hoped for a miracle.

*This can't last. Dad'll come to his senses. He'll miss us so much that any minute now he'll drive up in his car and get out as if nothing has happened. He'll hug Mum and then he'll hug me. He'll say he's sorry, it was all a big mistake.*

But he didn't.

The press picked up the story:

*Elizabeth Fielding – 'Dear Lizzie' to her thousands of readers – gives us no end of good advice but now seems to need it herself.*

Mum lost her cool and gave an interview. They printed a photo of her and Dad on their wedding day. The picture had been torn down the middle in ugly gashes. Nathan stared at it, biting his lip until he tasted blood.

Dad always arrived for lunch on Sundays with flowers or a cake. He took Nathan to the cinema, or to swim in the club pool. People came up to Dad and slapped him on the back.

"Hi, Max! Haven't seen you lately! This boy of yours is almost as tall as you!" Once they drove to Hertfordshire and walked for miles, the sky turquoise, the leaves turning.

Sundays flew. Nathan dreaded saying goodbye. He'd get home and listen to the quiet. He and Dad used to thump hilarious duets on the piano. Nathan didn't have the heart to play any more. None of Dad's friends telephoned. Mum stopped singing in the bath. Nathan turned up the TV to drown the silence and then sat with his fingers in his ears.

At half-term he went to stay with Dad and Karen for the weekend. "I really want you to meet her," Dad said. "She's been longing for you to come."

Mum took the Friday afternoon off and drove him to Primrose Hill. Bleak autumn rain hammered on the car. The windscreen wipers screeched against the glass. Mum parked in Elsworthy Road and peered out.

"That must be the house there. Dad said it had a green front door. They've got the top flat. They've both taken the day off work to welcome you. Karen's name will be on the bell. McBride. Her name's McBride."

Nathan reached for his bag, his legs like jelly.

"Have a great weekend. Dad will drop you home on Sunday night."

He watched as she drove away. *She's going to be on her own.* Pellets of rain bounced on to his face. By the time he turned towards the house, the door had opened.

"Nathan? Hi! I'm Karen." Her voice was low and smiley with a faint Scottish accent. "Delighted to meet you at last. Come in."

Karen was taller than Mum, almost taller than Dad as they stood together in the hall. She looked a lot younger than Mum, with curly red hair and pale skin with freckles. She had big hands and feet, and carefree green eyes that smiled like her voice.

Holding Dad's hand was a child with straight red hair tied into bunches which stuck out on either side of her head like giant shaving brushes. She looked coldly at Nathan and clutched a battered grey toy more closely, as if she were afraid he might snatch it.

"Hi, Nat!" Dad looked untidy and happy. "This is Amy ... Amy, this is Nathan. Say hello nicely now."

"Hi," Nathan said, forcing a smile. He could not bring himself to say her name.

Amy promptly hid behind Dad's legs.

Karen laughed. "She'll take a wee bit of time to get used to you ... Come on up."

The flat had big, sprawly rooms that nobody had

9

bothered to dust. "We thought you wouldn't mind sleeping in here." Dad opened the door to a room piled with junk. A sofa bed in the centre had been hastily covered with an old duvet.

"This'll be fine," Nathan said, but he woke in the night and couldn't remember where he was. Car headlights spun across the ceiling. His duvet had fallen off, his feet were freezing. He hauled the cover over himself, squeezed his eyes shut.

Dad's laughter bubbled through the wall.

In the morning, Nathan's door opened. Amy looked at him, still clutching her grubby grey toy. She wore white pyjamas patterned with red teddy bears.

"Go 'way, boy," she said.

"I'm not going anywhere," Nathan muttered. He sat up, pulling the duvet to his chin. "My dad's here and I want to be with him."

Amy curled her toes against the carpet. "*My* daddy," she said, and stuck a bright pink thumb in her mouth.

Later they went shopping at Sainsbury's. Amy sat in the trolley and made a mess with a choc ice. Dad and Karen kept meeting people they knew. "This is Nathan," Dad said, as if he were a stranger who happened to be in tow.

Karen cooked a casserole for lunch with lots of meaty

juices, and an apple crumble with a brown-sugar topping. "Super cook, isn't she?" Dad smiled in a silly secret way into her eyes.

Amy slid on and off Dad's lap as if he were a climbing frame.

They went for a walk on Primrose Hill and tried to fly a kite. It kept diving into the grass. Karen fell over into it and got knotted up in its strings. Nathan had never seen Dad laugh so much.

Early Sunday morning they left Karen in bed and went to the pool at Swiss Cottage. Dad spent all his time in the shallow end with Amy, teaching her to swim. In the afternoon they drove to Hampstead Heath. Amy fed the ducks on the pond. Nathan stared at her as she crouched at the edge, as Dad knelt beside her.

"If she says 'Go 'way, boy' to me again," he muttered under his breath, "I'll snatch her stupid little Eeyore and dump it in the pond."

That evening, Dad drove him back to the square. Outside the house, Nathan said, "Are you going to come in?"

The front door opened. Mum stood framed in the hall light.

Dad glanced towards her. "Another time," he said. He

hugged Nathan. "'Bye, Nat. We had a really great weekend, didn't we?"

Two nights before the end of term, snow fell. Not mizzly melting drops but huge triumphant flakes. By morning, the square stood hushed, transformed, the railings dazzling sentries, the beech trees bent under snowy pillows. Rooks marched stiffly on the drifts, arguing.

Nathan jabbed a fist at his window, startled by the whiteness and the quiet. He peered across at Tom's, shivered, and pulled on his thickest sweater. An hour later he was struggling down the street with Tom, kicking away the snow.

"Bad news, Banksie. The worst. Our party on December 23rd. I can't make it. It'll have to be at yours."

Tom ground to a halt. "You're *joking*. We've planned everything. Everybody'll be there. You can't back out now."

"I've got to go to Cornwall for Christmas." Nathan skidded into a snow drift. "Mum told me last night. I said I didn't want to go a hundred times. Useless. She won't listen."

"But we *always* have a party together." Tom pulled Nathan to his feet. "Couldn't you go to Cornwall for a few days and come back for it?"

"I suggested that. She says St Ives is too far and Grandpa's expecting us, specially for Christmas. Mum says he's lonely since Grandma died, but he managed without us last year perfectly well." He kicked at a lamppost. "First she plans the trip, then she tells me about it. I'm never asked about *anything*."

"Typical!" Snow speckled Tom's sandy hair like sugar on a cake.

"And for New Year, I'm going to Dad and Karen's again. I want to *see* Dad and all that, but it won't give you and me time to do anything."

Tom's eyes flicked over him, sympathetic. "That's OK."

"Come on, Banksie, it's *not* OK." The bus rumbled towards them, snorting waves of slush. "Mum's in a filthy mood. Karen's taking Dad to Edinburgh for Christmas to meet her family. I heard Mum telling Grandpa on the phone. She said it was the last straw and she can't wait to get away."

Tom followed Nathan to the back of the bus, where they squashed together in their usual seats.

"This isn't going to be a proper Christmas. I'll probably die of boredom." Nathan took off a glove, touched his left ear. "And I've got frostbite."

* * *

13

Nathan and Tom celebrated the end of term by building a giant snow pig in Nathan's front garden. It sat round and solid, with swirly pink marbles for eyes and orange peel for a smile.

"You're wicked." Nathan patted the pig's snout. "I can't bear to leave you. Perhaps it'll snow so hard tonight the roads to Cornwall will be blocked."

"Or you could catch a rare disease." Tom grinned. "Paint spots all over yourself. Demand to see a specialist."

"Brilliant idea. We can't leave the pig on his own for Christmas. All the snowmen in the neighbourhood will have him for bacon rolls!"

Mum opened the door. "I heard that. We'll get to St Ives tomorrow if we have to walk. Tom, give your mum my love. Nathan, come in and finish packing."

The door shut. Nathan threw a snowball at it. He looked at Tom and shrugged.

"Don't say anything." Tom brushed snow from his shoulders. "Ring me from St Ives ... Where are you staying?"

"Tregenna Castle. It's a hotel, huge and a bit grand. We've been there before. Usually we stay with Grandpa, but Mum says this time she wants a proper holiday without the chores."

Tom tried to look bright. "You can walk on the beach, watch the boats. It can't all be bad. Something amazing might happen." He punched Nathan's shoulder. "You might meet someone who'll change your life for ever, like in the movies."

Nathan pulled off his sopping gloves. "As if." His mouth puckered. "See ya, Banksie."

Tom skidded across the square. Outside his house he turned and waved, his face a weird yellow beneath the streetlight. Nathan flung an arm in reply.

He stamped into the house. The front room smelt stale, made him shiver. Last Christmas, he and Dad had put up a tree with silver-lantern lights, lit a log fire, sung carols round the piano. *Tomorrow Dad'll be in Scotland. Mum'll be with Grandpa.* He looked at the mound of snow in the front garden. *Piggy. That's what I'll be.*

*Piggy in the middle.*

He moved to the windowpane, blew warm breath on to it. Into its cloud he drew the word D A D. The letters began to dribble. He raised a sleeve to wipe them out. Through the clean circle of window a car drew up. A Ford.

Nathan skittered out of the room and flung open the front door.

"Hi, Nat!" Dad hugged him. He smelt of casserole.

"Thought I'd surprise you." He held a wicker basket full of parcels wrapped in shiny green paper. "I've brought you and Mum your Christmas presents. From me and Karen. And from Amy. She made you something special."

Nathan scowled. "What is it?"

"Aha! You'll have to wait until Christmas Day to find out!"

Mum emerged from the kitchen. "Hello, Max. Our presents to you are in that carrier bag." She hesitated at the doorway. "Are you taking Nathan for a meal?"

"So you knew Dad was coming?"

"Yes." Mum took the wicker basket. "Dad's got something he wants to tell you. I thought it might be best if you went out together."

A familiar cold sliver jabbed at Nathan's throat.

"The thing is ..." Dad drove through the snow towards the High Street. "We've all been so busy since the summer and our Sundays go so quickly." He glanced at Nathan. "I thought it would be nice to catch up a bit before we disappear to opposite ends of the country."

"I don't want to go anywhere." Nathan heard the sulk in his voice but he didn't care. "I'll miss my party with Tom for the first time ever. It's crap. Everybody wants to know why I can't be there."

"I'm sorry, it's partly my fault." Dad grated the gears. "I told Mum something that made her angry. I hoped she'd take it better." He ran a hand through his hair.

"*What* did you tell her?"

"Ah! Here's a good space to park." Dad reversed swiftly, hauled on the brakes and turned off the engine. He moved sideways to look at Nathan, flinging an arm along the edge of the seat. "It's about Karen. We've only just found out. She's going to have a baby. My baby. In July."

Nathan flushed. "She's already got Amy." Pause. "And you've got me."

"'Course I have." Dad touched Nathan's shoulder. "And I love you very much. You'll always be my special Nat." Pause. "But Karen and I, we're, you know, trying to make a life together."

Nathan opened his mouth, but the words wouldn't come out. He shoved at the car door and stepped with relief on to the pavement.

Dad joined him. "Let's go to that nice pizza place at the top of the hill. You're not crying, are you?"

"'Course not." Nathan hunched into his jacket and turned away.

The High Street sparkled with Christmas lights. They

hung over the street in showery spangles, turning patches of hardened snow deep pink and green. Crowds of people jostled their Christmas parcels, slithering excitedly up and down the hill. They brushed against Nathan, elbowed him out of their way.

Nathan fought back tears. *I'm not going to matter any more. A new baby. It'll be goodbye to Sundays with Dad when it arrives.*

In the packed restaurant, enormous pizzas frothed with cheesy topping. Nathan stabbed his with a fork, chewed desperately, made vast efforts to swallow. The cheese was slimy and the bread tasted of dust.

"Look." Dad ran his tongue over his lips. "I want to explain so you'll understand what this is all about. When my dad died, he left me a lot of money. Before you were born. I spent every penny on buying our house. I wanted somewhere big so I could have lots of kids." He pushed his hair out of his eyes, gulped at his wine.

Nathan stopped chewing. "You never told me that."

"No." Dad smiled at him, a strange smile full of shyness Nathan had never seen before. "It's not something men admit to. You can ask a woman what she wants in life and she can say marriage and children. But if you ask a guy, it's supposed to be money and promotion all the way."

"So when you met Mum, did you tell her?"

"That's a good question. I don't think I did, not in so many words. I already had the house, I kind of assumed she'd guess. We'd been married for three years before you were born." That smile again. "Happiest day of my life."

"Was it?" Nathan's lemonade fizzed in his mouth and stung his throat. "So why didn't you have more kids?"

Dad looked down at his plate. "Ask Mum."

"What do you mean? Didn't she want any more?"

"In a nutshell, no." Dad swirled the last of the wine around his glass. "She had her job on the newspaper and she had to be tough and committed and always in the office. I've never seen anyone work so hard. Part of me was pleased for her – she became a household name so fast. Another bit of me just wanted her to drop the whole thing."

"But she never did," Nathan said slowly. "I can't remember her not being at work."

"No. She'd made up her mind and there was nothing I could do to change it. At first she said maybe next year. Then I got straight refusals. Eventually I got fed up and I stopped asking her."

"But things are different with Karen?"

"The day I met her," Dad said proudly, "she told me about Amy and her divorce and how she'd always wanted more kids." He looked at Nathan, his eyes sharp. "She's good at her job, she enjoys it. But she's not ambitious. Her family come first. Amy – and now me. We'll always come first."

He took out his handkerchief, scrubbed his mouth with it. "You know what I feel?"

"No." Something inside Nathan steeled itself for another blow.

"Huge relief that I'm not competing with another career. That Karen and I can be a couple without her work coming between us all the time."

"I see." Nathan pushed his half-eaten pizza away. The babble of voices around him dinned into his ears.

"Do you?" Dad's eyes searched his face. "I want you to understand, to be a part of my new family. I want that more than anything."

Fresh overnight snow had buried their Volkswagen. Nathan scraped viciously at the windscreen. After ten minutes of coaxing, the engine sputtered into life.

"Thank the god of holidays for that!" Mum settled her beret more firmly on her head. "Off we go ... Great!"

"How can this be great?" Nathan hunched away from her as the car lurched out of the square. "I'm missing out on all the Christmas fun."

"We'll make up for it. Grandpa can't wait. He'll have tons of things planned."

"I don't *need* planning for. I can make my own plans ... I *like* making them."

"Sure, Nathan, but the point is, you can't live your own life yet. You and me, we're going to make some changes." She glanced at him. "Big ones."

"How big? What changes?" *Don't tell me. I don't want to hear.*

But he had no choice. Mum dropped her bombshell. She told him she was taking him to St Ives not just for Christmas, but because Dad was planning to sell their London house and she wanted to move back to St Ives for good. Just like that. Cool as a cucumber, driving along as if she didn't have a care in the world.

"I've thought about it a lot," she said, like she was chatting to a friend. "And frankly, I need a fresh start."

"Fresh *start?*" Shock pricked its way down Nathan's spine. He felt so flabbergasted he was almost speechless.

"I've never been a Londoner. Dirty, smelly city. But I've had to be here for my career. You'll love St Ives once you've settled down. My birthplace, my real home."

Nathan turned his head away so Mum couldn't see his face. *This is worse than anything. All my friends are in London. Dave and Steve, Lottie and Pippa ... Everyone at school, everyone who'll be at the party ... I'll never see any of them again.*

"You'll soon get used to the idea. We'll have great fun looking at cottages for sale."

Nathan wanted to shout, "Stop the car! Let me get out!" Instead he said in a deadpan voice, "And when exactly will all this happen?"

"Easter. We need time to sell the house and find you a new school. I've talked to my boss. She says I can write my weekly column anywhere. I'll travel up to the office once a month. It'll work perfectly." She paused. "I haven't told Dad yet."

"But I bet you've told Grandpa." Nathan's voice was icy

cold. "You're *bound* to have talked to *him*."

"Yes, I have." Mum sped past a gritter truck. "And now I'm talking to you."

Nathan shut his mouth and then his eyes. *Don't expect me to say another word.*

Driving west, the snow thawed, then vanished. Fields lay green against a dancing-cloud sky. The air loosened its icy grip, the traffic thinned. The silence between them thickened.

Near Exeter they stopped at a café, drank scalding tea and swallowed stiff Chelsea buns. A faint colour flushed Mum's cheeks. Nathan watched as she filled the car with petrol and bought acid-yellow chrysanthemums for Grandpa.

*She can't haul me off to Cornwall like this. I'm being hijacked. Christmas is one thing, but not for ever. She's got no right to take me away from Dad and Tom ... Cornwall's so boring.*

*Nothing ever happens there.*

They drove into St Ives at two o'clock, turning left at the signpost to Tregenna Castle. Giant firs shadowed the lawns and a golf course where neat miniature figures looked as if they were playing a board game.

Mum scooped off her beret. "We've made excellent time. Look, Nathan, the sea. Isn't this exciting? St Ives is down there, beyond the woods ... Remember?"

"Vaguely." *Leave me alone.*

Mum parked the car and Nathan climbed slowly out. He looked up at Tregenna Castle. Its massive grey walls, topped by turrets and a flag, seemed to lean towards him, as if they were surprised to see his face. The sun felt unexpectedly warm; the air smelt of salt and fir. A gull swooped from a turret, cackled at him mockingly.

He walked to the edge of the path and stared down at the woods that sloped towards the sea.

*I do remember. One morning. I was only three or four. I raced Dad down that path. I looked back at him and fell over. Dad picked me up. I made a big fuss. I'd cut my chin and grazed my hands and knees. Dad tied his handkerchief to my knee in a big white floppy bow. It made me laugh. Dad ... I want you with me now.*

Mum stood beside him. "Stunning, isn't it? We're going to have the best holiday in the world."

Nathan slouched away from her. *Best nothing. I just want to go home.*


He flung his bag on the floor and kicked it. The ground-level room, disgustingly clean, had an old-lady lavenderish smell.

Its windows faced earthy beds with shrubs, gravel paths, lawns. Outside, voices laughed and footsteps crunched.

He went to the window and looked across the woods to the flat blue blur of sea. A black liner crawled over the horizon like a determined beetle. *It's lucky. It's getting away.*

Mum put her head round the door. "Grandpa's here. Meet us in the lobby. I've ordered tea and sandwiches."

Nathan hurled himself on to one of the beds and bounced ruthlessly up and down on it. He pulled out two starched pillows, punched them, threw them venomously at the cupboard. They thudded against the slats and slumped to the floor. The cupboard door gaped open.

Nathan bounced until the bed groaned. "Come out, whoever you are!"

Empty coathangers jangled back at him.

He walked down the corridor, past the gym and its thunder of workout music. Past the long glass front of the swimming-pool, the excited splashing bodies. *If Dad were here, we could go swimming together. It's no fun on my own. I wonder what Tom's doing.*

Grandpa sat with Mum at one of the low tables in the lobby, clasping her hands. Nathan watched them awkwardly, not wanting to interrupt.

Grandpa spotted him. "Nathaniel!" He stood up. He was thinner, his face sharp and tanned. Thick white tufts of hair sprang back from his forehead. His moustache, bristling under his beaky nose, made him look like an elegant parrot.

Nathan hugged him. He smelt of Dettol and sherry.

Lively brown eyes inspected him. "You look more like Max than ever."

Nathan glanced at Mum. "I can't help that."

"Damn. Sorry, Elizabeth, dear. I didn't mean to put my foot in it."

Mum looked up at them, her eyes flicking from one to the other. "He is very like Max, though I never notice it ... Good. Here's our tea."

Nathan ate. Grandpa talked: the traffic, nowhere to park; the weird neighbours; the new supermarket. Nathan stopped listening. *I might as well not be here. Why couldn't she have left me on my own in London? I should have staged a sit-in at Tom's and refused to budge.*

But he listened again when Grandpa picked up his briefcase and pulled out a sheaf of papers. "I've done some legwork for you, Elizabeth. These arrived from Collins. He's the best estate agent in St Ives."

"Thanks, Dad."

"You haven't wasted much time, have you?" Nathan burst out.

Grandpa looked at him sharply. "Why, what's the matter?"

"What's the *matter*?" Nathan snorted. "Coming to live down here's the matter. It's the worst idea I've ever heard."

"Steady on –" Grandpa looked startled.

"I only told him about it this morning," Mum cut in, her voice cold. She tried to warm it. "If I make a few phone calls tomorrow, we could see some cottages at midday. How does that sound?"

"Crap." Nathan stood up. "I'm going to watch TV."

"Excellent." Grandpa gave him a hesitant smile. "Why don't you go for a swim before supper? You're a good strong swimmer, aren't you? Just like your dad."

Nathan glared at him and turned away.

"And tomorrow evening," Grandpa called, "we're going to the pantomime."

"That's *all* I need," Nathan muttered as he stomped back to his room. "I grew out of those stupid things years ago."

The screen's irritating flicker made Nathan want to kick it. He turned the TV off and picked up the phone. He told Tom about Dad's new baby, about the repulsively clean room, about Mum's decision. He could hear the shock in Tom's voice.

"Does your dad know?"

"Mum hasn't told him yet."

"Maybe when he knows he won't let her. He won't want you to live so far away."

"Do you think I should tell him?"

"Sure. Get him on your side."

"Right ..." Nathan began to plan the phone call in his head. An uncomfortable silence fell. "What's new with you?"

"We've put up decorations for the party." Tom seemed to search for something else to say. "And someone's been enjoying our snow pig. They jammed a row of Coke cans along his back. Made him look like a dragon."

Nathan forced himself to join in. "You mean a pragon."

"Or a drig."

They laughed.

"There isn't a bit of snow here. It's green and boring and ordinary." Nathan shut his eyes. He could see Tom sitting on the stairs, his legs draped over the banisters, the telephone balanced on his stomach. He missed him. He said quickly, "I'll ring again tomorrow, Banksie. Thanks for the advice. I'll take you up on it."

But when he dialled Dad's Edinburgh number, there was no reply.

In the morning, mist hid the woods and a steady rain fizzed against the window. By midday a reluctant sun had struggled through the clouds. Nathan slithered down the path through the woods with Mum. Tropical ferns dripped, the earth steamed, giant fir trees creaked.

At the end of the path a massive iron gate swung them on to the road. Nathan spotted figures in yellow oilskins on the beach, throwing sticks and chasing after their dogs, the wet sand splaying.

"Here we are." Mum pushed at the door. "Collins Estate Agents."

"Mrs Fielding?" A tall, fair-haired man stood up to greet them. "And this must be Nathan." He flashed huge white teeth. "I'm Collins Junior, but please call me Andy. We'll take my car – rather proud of it, new Rover 75. I've lined up three viewings."

*Smarmy git. Wish I were on the beach with a dog.*

"We should be able to whip round them pretty smartish ... Two in Carbis Bay. Then we'll take a peek at a house in Bowling Green Terrace."

They walked to the car park. The inside of the Rover

smelt of leather and cigarettes. Nathan sat in the back, glumly staring out .

Their first stop, a bungalow in Carbis Bay, looked as if it had been built for the set of a cheap American movie. Two dying palm trees wilted by the front door. The rooms jostled crazily patterned wallpaper and carpets. Nathan stood in a front bedroom. If he jumped, he could just see the edge of the coast from the window. Mum made excuses and they left.

The second, a house, squatted nearer the sea, reeking of damp. Its paint peeled, its greasy kitchen buzzed with old equipment.

At the Bowling Green Terrace house, set high in the centre of St Ives, a straggly garden flapped with grey washing. The rooms stank of dog. Nathan stood in the hall scowling at the floorboards. *Any minute now I'm going to run for the bus. I'll catch the first one I see and sit there until it gets to the end of its journey. Then I'll ring Tom and ask him to come and rescue me. I'll never come back. That'll teach Mum and her precious plans.*

They drove back to Andy's office. "Pop in again on Monday." He gripped their hands. "Tremendous pleasure to meet you both. *Do* take my card."

\* \* \*

"What a loser." Nathan clenched his fists until his nails bit into his palms. "And those dumps! I'd rather live in a tent."

They climbed the hill back to Tregenna.

"Don't worry, Nathan." Mum brushed a leather-gloved finger under his chin. He felt patronised, infuriated. "We'll find a wonderful place near the sea. Summer on the sands, swimming, cliff walking. It'll be marvellous."

"What *is* wrong with London? Tell me that. We can still have holidays. We've got everything. Your job. My ..." *Oh, what's the use? She's not listening.*

They reached the gate to the woods. Nathan picked up a stone and flung it into the stream. "Why d'you have to *destroy* everything?"

"Don't talk rubbish." Mum's voice hardened. "I'm starting again, rebuilding. It takes courage."

"That's a load of shit."

"Don't *use* that word."

"I'll use it if I like."

"Not to me, you won't."

At the top of the woods, hot, out of breath and now furious, Nathan kicked viciously at the edges of the grass. "When Dad left us, remember what you said?" His voice cracked. "You told me you'd promised Dad. That he and I'd stay close. How can I do that if we're down here?"

Mum turned her head away. "I know what I said. But that was in September –"

"So you're going back on your promise? I love our house!"

"Nathan." Mum seized his arm. "Strictly speaking, it's *Dad*'s house, and I told you he's decided to sell it. I'll get half the money. You know he wants a divorce. There's nothing I can do about that. What I can give us both is a new beginning."

Nathan wrenched away. "I don't *want* a new beginning. I don't want to go with you. Yes, Mum, no, Mum, anything you say, Mum. Coming for Christmas is bad enough. Being here day in, day out will be crap."

"How in heaven's name do you know until you've tried? Anyone'd think I was dragging you off to some ghastly dump instead of this beautiful place!" She swayed slightly, her cheeks yellowy white. "Come inside. Let's talk about this quietly."

Nathan backed away from her. "No. Let's not."

He turned towards the sea and sky, towards the freshening wind. "Talk to yourself. I'm going for a run."

"What about lunch? ... *Nathan!*"

His feet felt heavy. He willed them to move.

"Sod bloody stupid lunch," he shouted. "And sod you."

4

Nathan ran, he hardly knew where. Down the path, through the golf course, into the pine-tree shade, out on to the main road. He shot across it. Brakes squealed. A driver yelled at him, waving a fist. "Why don't you look where you're going, you stupid kid?" Another car screeched to a halt. More yelling. Nathan shouted back.

He ran on, shaking with fright and rage.

Turning away from the centre of St Ives, he found a narrow street dipping sharply to his left, and took it. At the bottom, he turned right and raced on. Houses stood further apart, their gardens aggressively tidy. Christmas holly, sparked with bright berries, hung from their gates. The noise of traffic faded.

Finally, Nathan reached the end of the road, a cul-de-sac. He stopped, short of breath, sweat pouring down his back. He bent to retie a lace on his trainers. As he straightened, he glanced at the cottage in front of him. It stretched long and low, grey stone, its small attic window half hidden in clambers of flame-red creeper. An apple tree curled bare branches.

And in the sudden quiet, something sang to him, a low murmur, a rhythmic splashing of waves.

*It's the sea, there, behind that cottage. I want to be near it.*

He glanced over his shoulder at the empty street. He unlatched the gate, walked towards the cottage. At the front door he stopped. No lights shone, no voices spoke. He ducked swiftly round the right-hand side into the back garden.

It seemed to sigh for him. It was filled with apple trees, beech and silver birch, warm and lush, with a magnificent abandoned wildness. Russet leaves shifted on the grass, winter roses shone like crimson candles. A black cat, crouching beside a stone pond, raised its head to inspect him, its yellow eyes alert.

Nathan darted through the trees. Rotting blackberry brambles snagged against his jeans. He glimpsed bits of his reflection in the broken windows of an old greenhouse. He ran on to the bottom of the garden, aware that the sound beneath the wind had become the clear thunder of sea. He reached the edge of the grass. He gasped.

Without warning the garden stopped, as if a giant hand had sliced the ground away. Below, slabs of moss-stained rocks met dark sand, splashes of glinting seaweed, a vast grey wash of sea and sky. The wind hummed into his ears, lifted his hair, threw fine sand on to his lips.

*Just look at that. Imagine being able to see that every day, in all different kinds of light and dark. I wish I had my sketchbook. Tom would love it here.*

At his feet he spotted metal footholds set into the cliff. He bent to look, almost began to climb, but something made him stay exactly where he was. Instead he squatted on the grass. His legs trembled, his heart raced. He licked his lips, tasting the sting of salt, the grit of sand.

He jumped. The cat had followed him, nudged against his hand. He dug his fingers into its thick fur, feeling its warmth, steadying himself. "Have you come to say hello?" The yellow eyes inspected him closely. "I nearly got run over. It was a close one! Had another row with Mum. I'm sick of it. The same old rubbish every time."

He looked down at the edges of the sea as they slapped sand.

Then he heard voices call to each other in a nearby garden. The sound cut through the air, jolted him into remembering what he was doing. Trespassing.

"I shouldn't be here." Reluctantly he stood up, brushed the damp grass from his jeans. "Better not get caught. Better get back."

He turned, feeling calmer, began to retrace his steps. He looked up at the cottage, at a second attic window.

Something was there.

Dead centre, motionless, black eyes stared out at him from a pale face and a mass of fair curly hair. The moment of light blurred, then faded. He tilted his head back, blinked and looked again.

Nothing, nobody.

The window must have reflected a cloud. It was a trick of light. It was a ghost.

He wanted to shout, *Come back! Who are you?*

Keeping behind the trees, he moved closer to the cottage. A crow cawed above him, beat its wings, flapped noisily into the sky.

He came closer still.

He heard a new sound. Crying. A girl crying. He moved up to the wall of the cottage. Sobbing, sobbing. Words he could not make out. Silence. He waited. The sobs began again, more quietly, equally wretched.

He scrabbled at a flower-bed, stood in the centre of the garden and threw a handful of earth at the window. He stared up, willing her to come.

She stood there again, her eyes black, her cheeks wet with tears.

He didn't dare to call. He mouthed, *"Can I help?"*

She shook her head, wiped a hand across her face.

"Please let me help." This time he spoke the words. "What's wrong?"

She struggled with the window and it shot open. "I knew you'd come." Her voice was high, bell-like, very clear.

He gasped "How did you –?"

"I just did, that's all. But you're too late."

"What for? How can I be –?"

"There's nothing you can do about it ... about anything. You shouldn't be here. Go away. Quickly, before he finds you."

He shivered as he stared up at her, noticed the pale shine of her skin; the necklace of jade-green stones at her throat; the long, slender fingers that pushed at her hair.

"Before *who* finds me?"

She mouthed, *"Be quiet!"* at him and reached for the handle of the window.

"OK, OK, I'm going."

He wrenched his eyes away. With a dull thud the window closed.

He made himself move, the girl's voice ringing in his head. His feet took him to the side of the cottage. A new sound greeted him. Hammering. It came from the front garden. It stopped, then started again.

Nathan hesitated. He edged towards the corner of the cottage wall and peered around it, bewildered.

A heavy, thick-set man, a dark green hat crammed over his head, thwacked at the top of a wooden post by the front gate.

Nathan's heart thudded. *What if he finds me here?*

He shrank back to the side of the cottage, listening. The hammering stopped. Footsteps crunched along the path and the front door slammed.

Nathan breathed again. He raced into the front garden and leapt over the low stone wall into the street. He looked back. From the wooden post fluttered a piece of paper with a handwritten message:

*For Sale, Cottage and Garden.*
*No Agents.*
*Ring 929363. Evenings Only.*

"Where *have* you been?" Mum hunched in the hotel lobby, defiantly stubbing out a cigarette.

"I went for a run."

"Well, I hope it put you in a better mood. I will *not* have you swearing at me, do you understand?"

Nathan nodded, not listening.

"Right. They've saved you some lunch. Dad rang from Edinburgh."

Nathan forced his thoughts away from the sound of sobbing which rang in his head. "Did you tell him about us moving down here?"

"Yes, I did. I told him there's no way I'm buying another house in London."

"What did he say?"

Her lips curled. "That I'd given him a lot to think about."

Nathan sat down, his legs numb. *So Dad won't put up a fight for me.*

"Don't look so gloomy." Mum tried to kiss him, but Nathan pulled away. "They've been decorating the Christmas tree. Isn't it pretty?"

Nathan glanced at the massive tree, its carefully arranged clutches of purple lights, the stiff gold fairy at the top brandishing a ridiculous wand.

"Great," he said bitterly. "I suppose they trot that lot out every year."

"At least they're making an effort. Come on, I'll keep you company while you eat. Tomorrow we're having lunch at Grandpa's. Proper Sunday lunch with all the trimmings. He's making an effort too."

\* \* \*

That afternoon, Nathan did his best to stop thinking about the girl. He swam in the pool, but the colours of the water flashed like the jade stones in her necklace. He walked across the golf course with Mum, comparing its flat dullness to the wildness of the cottage garden and the way it sliced down to the beach.

Back in his room, he got out his sketchbook and drew the cat crouching by the pond; the cottage, its windows empty and dark. He tried but failed to draw the girl's face. Her sobs echoed in his head like the mournful, insistent beat of a new pop song. He wished he could stop wondering who the man in the front garden had been, and why the cottage was for sale.

"Do I *have* to go to a kids' pantomime?" he grumbled that evening.

Grandpa brushed his complaint aside. "The St Ives Players are real professionals," he said firmly. "People book tickets months in advance and come from miles around. Trust me. *Mother Goose* will be wonderful."

Nathan sat glumly in the audience, listening in an absent-minded fashion to the excited buzz of voices around him. In front of the stage an enormous goose, painted on to the curtain in thick silver sparkle, flew into the sky, its one gold eye grinning at Nathan as if they were silent conspirators.

But once the curtain went up, in spite of himself, Nathan sat entranced. Both child and adult actors threw themselves into the simple storyline and strong music with energy and enjoyment. When the moment came, Nathan hissed and booed at the villain, screamed, "Oh, no, you're not!" as loudly as everyone else, and shouted with laughter at the hilarious antics of the goose.

In the interval he stood waiting to buy ice-creams. It was not until he had reached the head of the queue that he saw who was selling them. There was no mistaking those dark, anxious eyes.

He said, "Hi! I never realised it was you," startled by the sting of excitement that raced through him, the sudden thudding of his heart.

The girl recovered her poise but said nothing. Nathan lurched back to his seat, trying to balance three ice-creams. Half an hour later, he squinted over his shoulder. She stood at the back of the hall, gazing at the stage with rapt delight.

When he looked again, she had gone.

At the end of the show, Nathan pushed outside ahead of Mum and Grandpa. He stood in the jostling crowd, hoping to see her. When he did, a sudden shyness gripped him. She caught his eye, but rapidly looked away. She was obviously waiting for someone, he told himself sternly. He could hardly barge up to her ...

The crowd thinned. Grandpa and Mum talked with friends. Nathan watched as some of the child actors emerged, one of them holding the goose's costume. The girl bobbed towards them. He heard her say, "You were great!" There was talking, laughing, general congratulations. The group moved away. The girl, on its edge, seemed to hesitate. Then she ran off alone in the opposite direction.

Nathan was suddenly desperate to follow her, but Grandpa's voice cut through the crowd. "Nathaniel? Come and meet some friends of mine."

And the moment was lost.

When he woke next morning, Nathan's plan of action was fully formed, as if it had hatched in the night like a gosling, pecking with determined single-mindedness through its fragile shell.

Grandpa lived high in the centre of St Ives, in the same terrace as the house he and Mum had seen yesterday.

*The last time I stood here, Dad was with us, and Grandma was alive. I was eleven. It was summer. Why does everything have to change?*

"Elizabeth! Nathaniel! Come in, come in." Grandpa was wearing a striped apron and his hair stood fiercely on end. The fragrance of roast lamb wafted into the hall.

Lunch was delicious. Nathan was surprised and pleased. "You're not just a pretty face, Gramp." He grinned across the table.

"Oh, I *know*." Grandpa met Nathan's eyes. Laughter linked them. "Well, if Grandma could do it, I said to myself, why can't I? Coffee, Elizabeth?"

He darted into the kitchen. Mum disappeared to the loo.

Nathan saw his chance. "I'm off," he called to an empty room. "I won't be long."

He flung on his coat, slipped out of the house and raced down the hill, his arms flying.

The town vanished beneath his feet. He ran up the hill to Tregenna, past the woods, along the road until the left turning. Down, right, left and down again.

But when he reached the cul-de-sac, he knew at once he'd have to think again.

A young woman with a baby on her back stood in the front garden of the cottage with the tall, thick-set man Nathan had seen the day before. He wore jeans, a heavy fisherman's sweater, the same dark green hat with a floppy brim. He held a file of papers and pointed at the roof.

Nathan walked towards them, but as he drew closer they nodded to each other and disappeared into the cottage. The front door clicked and a light flickered.

Nathan cursed. He pulled an old biro from his coat pocket and wrote down the 'for sale' number on the inside of his wrist. Then he walked out of the cul-de-sac.

*Now what do I do?*

He heard Dad's voice in his head. *"I'd go straight back to Grandpa's if I were you. At this very moment they're wondering where on earth you've gone."*

*I'm allowed out on my own. I'm not a kid.*

*"Sure, Nat, but that's hardly the point. That girl you saw – OK, she was obviously upset. But it's none of your business, is it? You can't invade other people's lives just because you're curious about them."*

Nathan squared his shoulders, his determination sharpened. *Can't I just!*

He'd go down to the beach and find the cliff with the metal footholds. He could get into the garden that way and try to find the girl.

He ran through the streets to the main road, raced on, down the steps to Porthminster Beach. His boots sank into the sand.

The beach stretched long and deserted. It curved in on itself, the rocks almost closing it off, then opened out into a smaller cove, and then another. Rock pools slurped at his feet. He slithered and climbed as fast as he could.

He looked up at the cliffs to get his bearings. At the top, on the corner furthest from him, stood a figure in scarlet trousers and a black jacket. Its pale face stared out to sea. The fair curly hair whipped back in the wind.

*It's her.*

He waved but she made no response. He lowered his head, quickened his pace, strode away from the sea towards her. He stared up again. The man stood beside her, his green hat crammed over his head. It looked as if he were shouting at her, menacing her, threatening.

She stared ahead. Then she turned to face him, raised her fists, flailed at him. He caught her wrists and flung her arms to her sides. Something white fluttered to the ground. She turned, ran back towards the cottage. The man followed.

The wet sand made it hard to move fast. Nathan bent his

head and lunged forwards, pulling as quickly as he could towards the cliff. It rose away from him, sharp and steep. He scanned it for the footholds and spotted glints of metal. The ladder snaked above him.

He grabbed the first foothold, frightened it might not take his weight. It felt deadly cold but stayed locked in place. He started to climb. His feet skidded on the rungs and he told himself to slow down. Gradually his climbing gained rhythm. As he moved he saw a changing landscape: the flow of coves, the long ribbon of sea, the surly, darkening sky.

The ladder came to an abrupt end on a small plateau. He crawled on to it, feeling the sandy grass beneath his chin, fighting to catch his breath. A pair of gulls screamed away from him.

With a fierce swoop, the cliff rose again to the garden's edge. Nathan climbed the last few rungs, clung to the surface and looked towards the cottage.

The girl and the man had gone.

Something lay crumpled on the grass. Nathan reached for it: a handkerchief, soft, white, bordered with creamy lace. It smelt weird. He held it to his nose. Oil paint, high and pungent, and something else, sweet and heavy, like honey. He turned the fragment of linen in his hand. An initial coiled in the corner, embroidered in deep yellow thread. The letter *R*. He traced his fingers over it.

Thunder grumbled the first few drops of rain. Startled, he stuffed the handkerchief into his pocket, stood up and ran into the garden. A light shone from the attic window. He stared up at it.

The man stepped from behind one of the trees. Nathan's heart kicked.

"Who the hell are you?" The man's eyes loured at him, black, heavy-lidded.

Nathan ducked away from him.

"Not so fast." The man grabbed his arm, slammed him against a tree. He stood head and shoulders above him, thick-set and powerful. "This is a private garden. What are you doing here?"

"I was on the beach," Nathan jabbered. The weight of the man's hands gave him no room to manoeuvre. "I slipped on a rock, twisted my ankle. I needed a quick way home."

"And the quickest way was up our cliff!" The man tightened his grip, shoved his face close to Nathan's. He stank of beer. "I don't think so." The words slurred into each other. "There's nothing wrong with your ankle, you stupid little liar. Clear off before I call the police. And no more tricks, d'you hear? Next time I'll make sure you *never* get away."

Nathan wrenched himself free and crashed across the grass. Sharp fingers of rain stabbed his neck. In the front garden he ran backwards, looking up at the attic window.

A hand pressed against the pane.

Nathan slammed the door behind him and glared at the hotel room. It stared back, clean, blank and cold. He flung his wet coat on the floor.

*I've had enough of this nightmare. I'm going to hitch a lift to London and then to Edinburgh. I'll talk to Dad, see if I can come and live with him.*

It took him five minutes to pack. His bag sat on the bed, bulging and zipped. *But first I'll ring Dad and tell him I'm coming.* He reached for the phone. *He'd just better be there, that's all. If he's out, I'm off, and I'll think about it later.*

His fingers shook as he poked at the dial.

"Hi, Nat." Dad's voice sounded a million miles away. "How's tricks?"

"Fine," Nathan lied. "I've swum in the pool, walked on the beach." He swallowed. "How's Edinburgh?"

"We had a terrible journey, what with the traffic and the snow. Amy was sick and Karen got really worried about her."

"Is she OK?" *Amy! Why are we talking about that smarmy brat? What about me?*

"She's fine, but she's not a good traveller. I'd forgotten how much attention a tiny tot needs!"

"I need attention too." The words spilt out of him.

"'Course you do, Nat. Next year I'll make it up to you. You must come to us and we'll have the best Christmas ever."

"You'll have a new baby by then."

"All the more reason for you to come. He'll be your brother."

"Half-brother. Or half-sister." Nathan hated the sound of the words.

"Quite right. Isn't it exciting? ... So, how's Mum?"

Nathan took a deep breath. "You know she wants us to live down here?"

"Yes, she told me yesterday. I mean, I know we need to sell the house, but her decision came as a bit of a shock. I'd no idea she was planning to move back to Cornwall."

"You and me both." Nathan's voice cracked. *Ask him, ask him, you have to ask.* "Couldn't I live with you, Dad? I'd really fit in well. I'll do anything to help."

*Please, Dad, please. Say yes.*

"Oh, Nat." Dad sighed. "That's got to be out of the question, so don't even think about it."

"But I could come to see you now, Dad. It wouldn't take

long. I could hitch a ride. Then we could talk about it properly."

"That's a crazy idea." Dad's voice sounded louder, urgent. "Mum would never let you go. You mustn't do anything like that. It'd really upset her. Please, Nat, promise me. Promise you'll stay with her. Say it now, I promise."

Nathan forced out the words. "I promise."

"Good lad. Be sensible. We'll make lots of plans for the holidays. Half-terms. And of course, after Christmas, we're going to ... We'll write down firm dates for the diary. Be patient, that's all I ask."

In the background Nathan heard Karen calling. A frosty hand clutched at his heart.

"I must go," Dad said. "Love you loads. Take care of Mum. We *all* love you, you know. Speak to you soon."

"Dad –" Nathan said, but the line died.

He wanted to pull the phone out of its socket and throw it through the window. Instead he grabbed at his packed bag, unzipped it, hurled its contents one by one around the room. Then he sat for a long while, staring at the mess.

*Dad doesn't want me any more. That's the truth, so why don't I just face up to it?*

He forced his arms to push him from the bed. He bent, picked up his wet coat. He fished in one pocket, then in the other. From it he drew out a small white lace-edged handkerchief. He clenched it in his fist.

The scent of oil paint and honey lifted into the air.

"Can I go into St Ives?" He and Mum finished breakfast in the dining-room. *Invent an excuse. Anything to get away from this hotel.* "I want to buy Gramp a Christmas present."

Mum looked at him over her teacup. "OK, but don't *completely* disappear off the face of the earth like yesterday. One minute you were there, the next no Nathan for hours and you turn up soaked to the skin. Gave us quite a scare. Grandpa was pacing the kitchen like a caged lion."

"I'm not a kid. I can go off on my own if I want."

She put down the cup. "He *cares* about you, Nathan. You're his only grandchild."

Nathan gazed at the tablecloth. "That's not my fault."

"I tell you what. I'll meet you for a Coke at eleven. Sharp, mind. I don't want to spend the morning worrying about you. Is that clear?"

"Yeah." *What a pain. I'd really like the day on my own.*

"Go down to the waterfront. Walk to the end of the Wharf. Fish Street leads off it. Kathy's Bar's about halfway along. I'll see you there."

"Right." Nathan looked at her. "May I have some pocket

money, please? Last week's *and* this?"

"Sorry, Nathan, I completely forgot. I must owe you tons." She rooted in her bag. "Here. Special bonus."

"Thanks," he said without much feeling. He put the crisp notes in his pocket.

"By the way. Your Christmas present. Grandpa wants you to choose something special." She smiled at him. "Have a look around. Something might take your fancy."


He pulled on a thick-ribbed sweater and a scarf, and checked his jeans. Money, the oil-paint-and-honey handkerchief. He raced down the corridor, out of the hotel.

*Freedom!*

In the woods, sunlight flecked through the firs. A squirrel spotted him, its paws clamped to its mouth. It rippled towards a tree, its tail flying like a flag on a grey boat. Nathan reached the end of the path, opened the gate and crossed the road to be nearer the sea, the sound of its swirling roar. *It's like having a new friend.*

He ran down the hill to the metal steps leading on to the beach, clattered down them and crunched across the pebbly sand to the shoreline's edge. The sea sucked and heaved to its own insistent rhythms, splashing his boots, filling his ears with its great welcoming sighs.

He crouched, his elbows on his knees, looking out across the grey waters to the soft ripple of coves.

"Hi," he said. "I'm Nathan. Looks as if we'll be seeing a lot more of each other."

He pulled off his gloves and reached for a handful of pebbles. They smelt of salt and tar. One by one he threw them, cold and wet and smooth, into the sea.

He stood up.

"Don't go anywhere," he said. "I'll be back."

He walked swiftly down the narrow streets, peering into shop windows. He bought Grandpa a cookery book, Mum an orange woollen scarf. As he crossed the road by the church he caught sight of Grandpa scurrying along, carrying a small fir tree. Nathan hesitated. He could offer to help but that would be the end of the morning on his own. Instead he ducked out of sight and ran down to the waterfront to watch the boats bumbling on the shore.

And then cool fingers seemed to stroke the back of his neck. He spun round.

The girl was walking swiftly past the harbour shops. She wore the same scarlet trousers and black jacket. She was carrying a parcel, her head bent over it. She stopped outside the art shop and vanished inside.

Nathan spurted across the street. He reached the shop and pushed at the door. The bell clanged. A familiar scent wafted towards him: oil paint but with a rougher base, a mix of wood, paper and canvas. Watercolours in boxes stacked in pyramids next to bulging tubes of oil paint. Bristling brushes like baby hamsters peered over the shelves at pencils with tips as sharp as pins.

"Morning, Charlie."

The voice from the far end of the shop called to Nathan like a bell. He ducked behind a shelf.

"I've brought you two more paintings."

"Rosalie." A man's voice, deep, with a rich burr. "Good to see you."

"Here ..." Rustle. "Do you like them? The paint's hardly dry on that one."

"Very much." Chuckle. "I recognise *that.*"

"I thought you might! ... Could you sell them for me?"

"I'll certainly do my best. Trade's pretty brisk at the moment, what with Christmas."

"Thanks, Charlie." More rustling. "What are you doing?"

"Giving you these watercolours for Christmas."

"Oh ... " Nathan heard the voice catch for a second. "You're one in a million."

Nathan inspected a box of chalks as if he were reading the works of Shakespeare. He dared not look round. He listened as the footsteps reached the door. Then he spun round and out of the shop.

The girl had turned right. She walked fast, down the harbour road, her hair bouncing. Her trousers were streaked with paint. Nathan followed, his stomach clenched into a ball of fire.

*What am I doing, Banksie? Chasing after a girl!*

*"Great stuff, Weed. Go for it!"*

*But what if I catch up with her? What'll I say?*

*"Tell her about yesterday, that you went back specially to see her."*

*Right. I'm so near I could touch her. If I reach out, I could tap her on the shoulder.*

The girl raised her arm suddenly and waved. Two tall fair-haired boys shouted a greeting from the waterfront. She stepped off the pavement and ran towards them.

Nathan stopped. He looked over at the small group, reminded that he had no friends here, jealous of the way they talked and laughed. Downcast, he turned away.

*I don't believe this. So near and yet –*

*"Yeah, yeah, so far! Come on, Weed, get your act together. Have you still got that 'for sale' number?"*

Nathan checked the inside of his wrist.

*"Right. Now tell me what you're going to do next."*

*I'm going to meet Mum, get her to ring it.*

*"And just remind me why."*

*Because maybe if I can get inside that cottage I can meet that girl. Face to face.*

Mum sat by the window of Kathy's Bar. She waved. Nathan stepped into the scent of freshly ground coffee.

"I bought you a Danish pastry and a Coke," Mum said. "OK?"

Nathan sat down. "Thanks."

"When you've eaten, I thought we might do some more estate agenting."

"Yeah." Nathan straightened his shoulders. "Thing is, I've been thinking –"

Mum flushed. "You're not going to start arguing again, are you? I really couldn't bear –"

"No, you've got it wrong. OK, I *didn't* want to move. I *am* still thinking about it. But the thing is, I found a cottage. On Saturday."

Mum choked into her coffee. *"What?"*

"I wasn't *looking* for anywhere. I was running and I stopped to catch my breath. There's a 'for sale' note pinned on a wooden post."

"Well, I'll be —"

"I haven't been *inside*. I kind of like it. I mean, I think it's worth looking at."

"I'm gobsmacked."

"The back garden, it *probably* goes down to the sea. You can't hear traffic or anything. It's very quiet." He bit into the pastry.

"Nathan Fielding, you astonish me ... This 'for sale' note, was there a phone number on it? Did you by *any* chance write it down?"

"I might have done." He checked the faint blue scribble along the veins of his wrist and read it out. He grinned. "Well, what are you waiting for?"

Mum leaped across the café to the corner phone.

Nathan demolished the pastry and drank the Coke. He stared out of the window, thinking about Rosalie. He knew her name now. It suited her, had a kind of ring about it, like her voice. She might walk by, her hair flying in the wind, her face intent, watchful.

If she did, he'd jump up and race out — and this time, he wasn't going to let her get away. He'd throw himself in front of her and say he'd tripped. And she'd say, "Hi! Haven't I seen you before? Of course! You're the boy in the garden!"

Then he'd ask her how she'd known he'd be there and

why he'd been too late? What had he been too late for? Who was that bloke by the cliff? And she'd smile and say, "All in good time," and they'd walk together, down to the waterfront and on to the beach. And then –

"There's no reply." Mum slid back into her chair. "I tried twice. Are you sure it's the right number?"

"I've just remembered. The note said ring in the evening."

Mum's shoulders sagged. Then they revived. "We could walk there and see the place from the outside."

"That's a great idea. Can I drop these parcels at Tregenna?"

Mum stood up, looking young and energetic. "Lead on, explorer."

They stood at the top of the cul-de-sac.

"There it is. Right at the end." He couldn't keep the pride out of his voice.

"Wow. I see what you mean."

They walked towards it, stood looking at the front garden. Nathan skimmed the windows. No sign of Rosalie. Perhaps she was still in St Ives.

"It's a pity we can't see the back garden," Mum said. "I wonder what it's like."

Nathan clenched his fists in his pockets. One of them closed over *R*'s handkerchief.

"Can I help you?" A sharp voice challenged them from a nearby garden. A tiny woman in a blue knitted dress and slippers stared at them. She clutched her gate with pink rubber-gloved hands as if she were steering a ship into harbour.

Mum turned. "I wonder if you can. We're in St Ives for a few days to see my father. We're from London, but we want to move down here. My son, Nathan, spotted this cottage. I rang the number but nobody answered."

"No, they wouldn't, not until tonight." The woman inspected them more closely. "Just thought I'd check. You can't be too careful these days and he asked me to keep an eye out. But if you're seriously interested in buying, I've got a key. I could show you round, Mrs – ?"

"Fielding. That would be most kind of you. We've so little time, what with Christmas and then we're off home on Boxing Day. Are you sure it's convenient?"

The woman smiled. "My name's Martha." She peeled off the gloves, which burped beneath the strain. "Won't be a tickety split."

She shuffled off.

Nathan bit his lip, turned away and kicked a stone

across the street. Maybe his plan to get into the cottage was a totally bad idea. The girl had her own life. One of those boys on the waterfront just now was probably her boyfriend. She couldn't possibly be interested in him.

But his heart lurched. The hair on the back of his neck stirred as if it needed somewhere else to grow. He spun round, craned up at the attic. For a fleeting moment he saw the anxious eyes, the hair.

Then they vanished.

"There you go, no problem." Martha now wore a pair of high-heeled shoes in which she tottered like a baby sparrow. "My word, what a lovely morning. Isn't this *fun?*" She unlocked the front door and opened it wide. "Please, do come in."

*Rosalie's in the attic. Soon we'll be face to face.*

Eagerly, Nathan pushed across the threshold.

The hall looked like the inside of a painted cave. On his left stretched a mural of a beach, painted in vast washes of blues, greens and biscuit yellows. Pale clouds chased over the horizon, the sand gleamed. At the sea's edge, two figures flew an orange kite. It rode the sky like a triumphant bird.

Opposite hung a portrait of a woman, her eyes green, her hair pulled from her face. Blue curtains brushed the floor. Winter roses stood on a table, their petals curling. A dish of pebbles clustered next to them, like speckled eggs.

"It's a magic grotto," Nathan said.

"Wow," said Mum. "This is beautiful."

"I'm afraid it's only the hall now," Martha said. "When Moira – *Mrs* Croft – was alive, the whole house was beautiful. She was a painter, real talented. Her daughter takes after her. Sweet girl, always so polite. Now Mrs Croft's passed on – it happened the summer before last, that's right, eighteen months ago – my, how time flies. Terrible, it was. We were all shattered. Well, *he's* let the place go to the dogs, if you don't mind my saying. I've got high standards, me, can't bear filth. Dust top to bottom every day, hoover every other." She ran a finger along the wooden banister and revealed the grimy result. "But Jake – *Mr Croft* – he doesn't seem to notice. 'Course, some men don't, and he has had rather a lot on his plate lately."

"Is Jake Croft the owner?" Mum asked.

"Yes, indeed. Hung on living here for as long as he could – or so he says. To tell you the truth, I don't think his heart's been in it since Moira died. I'd have fought tooth and claw to keep a cottage like this, but Mr Croft, he – well, I'd better not say too much. I never like to gossip. He's been out of work and I reckon the bills just got too much for him."

"Right," Mum said briskly. "Could we wander around? See the garden perhaps?"

"I'm terrible once I start chattering." Martha clattered across the hall into a long, low room with French windows. "It's *gorgeous* out the back. I'll open these glass doors for you. There's a *wonderful* view at the end. Do please come in."

The room felt abandoned. Books clumped about in corners although their shelves had been removed. A few paintings hung lopsidedly on the walls: a field burning with poppies, a beach soaked in rain. Two leather sofas had gathered shabby pink cushions. A slate fireplace spilled half-burned logs into the grate and a lingering scent of firewood hung in the air.

"This is a lovely room," Mum said. "Needs a lick of paint, that's all."

A black cat stood at the windows, arching its back. It made straight for Nathan and curled around his legs.

"Well, I *never!*" Martha gaped "That's our Tiggy. It's like she *knows* you. You must have a real knack with animals!"

Nathan bent to stroke her. "Hi, Tiggy. So *that's* your name." A blackberry bramble caught at her neck. Gently he pulled it away. She ducked against him, purring.

"*Amazing* ... Well, young man – Nathan, is that right? I'll show your mum the garden. We can have a little chat about the price." She paused. "Since you've scored such a hit with our Tiggy, why don't you go and explore?"

Mum nodded to Nathan. Immediately he left the room and began to climb the stairs.

The enchantment of the hall swiftly disappeared. The grey carpet was threadbare; in places, patches of wooden boards glimmered through apologetically. The rooms on the first floor had also been partly stripped of furniture and a tap dripped insistently from the bathroom.

A second flight of stairs, made of pine and covered in

dust, led up to the attic. Nathan hesitated, listening to the quiet. He ran a hand through his hair, wondered nervously whether his face was clean. He tiptoed up the stairs. At the top, a door blocked his way.

He tapped on it gently, his hammering heart making more noise than his knuckles. He waited, pushed at the door and stepped inside.

The attic stretched stark and spacious, cluttered and empty, dancing with spidery shadows. Sunlight poured through the windows, filling the room with arcs of golden dust. Its wooden floor threw up spatters of paint. Wide shelves creaked with canvases, paints, bottles, brushes and books. Two battered armchairs slumped in the centre, next to an easel with sketches of a child. Long curtains fell heavily to the floor.

A desk crouched near the window that overlooked the back garden. On it lay a painting: two shadowy people, a man and a woman, walked along a beach, pushing against the wind, the sky behind them dark with thunderclouds, the sea full of angry foam. A set of watercolours gleamed wetly in the sunlight, and a brush, dipped in a jar of water, seeped a deep grey.

Nathan moved closer. The water swirled.

Slightly, with a sigh, one of the curtains swelled.

Nathan froze. Without raising his head, he swivelled his eyes to it, then down towards the floor and the tips of two red leather shoes. He reached out and drew back the curtain.

The girl stared out at him. Anger, fear and then relief washed across her face. "You're the boy in the garden."

"Yes." He could hardly speak.

"Nobody else knows I'm here." Her voice was low, the words rapid, anxious. She smeared a hand over her forehead, leaving a trail of grey paint. "Don't dare give me away."

"You know I won't."

He stepped back, looking at her. Her eyes were not black but an extraordinary dark blue. Her fair hair, streaked with paint, curled to her shoulders. She wore a long purple sweater over scarlet trousers, the same silver necklace with oval jade-green stones. Her skin seemed to shimmer with light.

*You're the most fantastic girl I've ever seen.*

"I came back to see you yesterday." Suddenly he couldn't get the words out fast enough. "But that bloke was in the front garden with a woman and a baby. When I got to the beach I saw you with him. I climbed the cliff into the back garden. I saw your light on, but then he spotted me. Almost beat me up ..." He swallowed. "I've got your handkerchief."

He pulled it from his pocket and held it out to her. "This morning, I saw you again. In the art shop. I followed you, but you ran to meet your friends."

She looked at him silently, her lips curling, almost as if she had heard it all before.

"Was one of them your boyfriend?" He was dying to know.

"No." She blushed. "I haven't got one. They're just friends of mine from school."

"Your name's Rosalie, isn't it?"

That startled her. "How do you know?"

"I heard the man in the shop. I'm Nathan. Nathan Fielding." He clenched his fists and ploughed on. "Why were you crying?"

"None of your business." She snatched the handkerchief. "I've got to finish this painting."

Nathan looked it more closely. "It's great. Those people on the beach – the way they're being blown by the wind and you can't really see their faces."

"It's been the hardest thing to get right. I have this dream ... But I don't even know –" She broke off, as if she had begun to tell him something important but had changed her mind.

"Just now ... why were you hiding?"

Anger flashed in her eyes. "I shouldn't be here any more, not now this cottage is for sale. Except I'm desperate for the money and I've nowhere else to work."

"Why?" He felt a burning curiosity about her, wanted to know every detail of her life, every minute of her past.

"The flat Dad's renting, it's over the fish and chip shop on the waterfront – there's no space, is there? No room for anything." She bit her lip. "Why don't you leave me in peace to get on with this while I still can?"

"I only want to help."

"No, you don't. You're just being nosy." She tore at the lace edges of the handkerchief and threw it on the desk. "Anyway, you're too late. If you'd come before he ... before all this happened, maybe you could've –"

She looked out of the window and her body stiffened. "Who's that in the garden with Martha?"

"My mum."

"Lucky you!"

"What do you mean?"

"I haven't got a mother any more." Her voice was bitter. "*I* have to manage without one –"

"I know." He bit his lip. "Martha ... when she let us in ... she told us ... I'm sorry."

The girl seemed to shy away from sympathy, as if she couldn't bear it. "What's your mum *doing* with Martha?"

"We've come down from London." Sweat broke on Nathan's top lip. "For Christmas. My grandpa lives here."

"So?" She glanced at him impatiently.

"Mum's planning to sell our house in London and buy somewhere down here. I saw the notice in your garden –"

"And I thought you might be different!" The girl flushed. "I should've known! You and your mum, you're nothing but vultures." She turned away from him and sat abruptly at the desk. "You can't wait to get at the pickings, can you?"

"That's not fair!"

She reached for the paint brush, but her hand shook. "You're the third lot so far. There was a stupid fat woman with a baby yesterday. The day before some posh couple turned up, all lah-de-dah and two smelly Labradors. The cottage hadn't been for sale for more than half an hour. Said they'd just been out for a stroll! This is my home we're talking about. I was *born* here. This attic was Mum's special place, hers and mine."

She put down the brush, scraped her fingers through

her hair. She picked up an elastic band and tied back the curls. Nathan gazed at the pale furry skin on the back of her neck. He had to stop himself reaching out to touch it.

He swallowed. "Don't you want to sell this cottage then?"

"Want to? *Want to?*" Her voice rose. "I begged him not to –"

"Who?"

"Pleaded. I'd do anything Would you want to sell this place if you lived here?"

"Well, I –"

"Just don't ask stupid questions." Her shoulders drooped. "It makes everything worse."

"Sorry." Nathan backed away from her and perched stiffly on the arm of a chair. "I'm trying to make things better, but nothing I say is any use."

She gave a short laugh. "If you want to be *useful* you can go ... And don't bother to come back ... You *and* your mum. Tell her to get lost ... Just like mine."

"OK, OK, I get the picture." Nathan stared at the floor's snake-like spatters of paint. It occurred to him that even though his mum was infuriating, having her around was probably better than not having a mum at all. Almost against his better judgement, he persisted. "How did it happen? Your mum?"

"I never talk about it." Her voice was sullen. "Not to anybody. So why should I tell you?"

"It's what friends are for," Nathan began lamely, but she was having none of that.

"You're not a friend, you're a buyer. You came snooping round the cottage because you knew it was for sale –"

"That's not true! I'd no idea. I'd had a row with Mum and I'd run away from her. I found this cottage quite by chance, heard you crying, wanted to help." He stood up, his legs shaking with indignation. "And you couldn't possibly have known I was going to be here."

"Ah, but I did." She wheeled round in her chair, her eyes blazing. "I can see things in my head. Things nobody else can see, before they happen."

"Like me being in the garden?"

"Yes. And bad things too … Like Mum's accident. That was the worst so far." Tears glittered in her eyes but did not fall.

"You mean you knew about it before –"

She turned her face away. "I told you, I don't want to talk about it. It makes everything worse."

Nathan tried desperately to think of something to say. "What about your dad? Didn't he help? Couldn't he have –"

"*Him*." Her voice took on a new harshness. "He was in

France when Mum died ... Anyway, you've already met him."

"Have I?"

"The man in the green hat?"

Prickles of frost ran down Nathan's spine. "That bloke in the garden was your dad? The one who nearly beat me up?"

"Mastermind." Her short, high laugh sounded like a cry.

"You mean he's really violent?"

"Only when he's drunk." Pause. "Which is most of the time these days."

He noticed her wrists. "Those bruises." The skin flushed dark pink and grey. "Did he do that to you?"

"We were arguing," the girl said abruptly. Voices drifted from the garden. She seemed glad of the interruption. She pulled her sleeves down and glanced out of the window. "Martha's coming in with your mum. She's bound to come up here. I'll have to hide again." She stood up and slid behind the curtain. "Don't let on. Do you hear?"

"I'll get rid of Mum. But I can't leave you here like this."

"You *must!*" Her voice was muffled.

"I can't just stand by and –" Panic pumped through him. "We've got to talk. Afterwards. Promise."

"Nathan?" Mum's voice called from the floor below, then at the top of the stairs. She walked into the attic.

"Wow. What an amazing room." She stood in an arc of sunlight. "They must use this as a studio. Look at the view."

"Yes." He stood with his back to the curtain.

"Talk about beginner's luck. The garden's paradise. It dips straight down a cliff to the sea." She flopped into an armchair, her face shiny with happiness. "This is a miraculous find of yours, Nathan. It must be fate. I can *feel* us living here."

"Yes." *I must get her out of the attic.* "Is that Martha calling you?"

"Is it? I didn't –"

"She probably wants us to leave –"

"Quite right. We shouldn't take up any more of her time." On the stairs she turned. "I'll ring Mr Croft tonight from Tregenna and make him an offer. I can't wait to tell Grandpa. He'll be over the moon." She disappeared.

"That's it, isn't it?" the girl hissed. She flung back the curtain. "I'm done for. The vultures have circled and now they're going to swoop."

"Don't *talk* like that. You make me feel so guilty ... When can I see you again?"

"Haven't a clue. Does it matter?"

"Yes. It does to me."

She shrugged, her face pale.

"I'm going to come again ... as soon as I can get away."

He turned towards the stairs and glanced back at her. She was staring down at her painting, her arms clenched around her body as if for comfort. He wanted to hug her.

On the landing, he thought of a plan. He unwound his scarf. He'd leave it in the kitchen. Then, just as he and Mum were leaving, he'd make it an excuse to dash back and find it.

He'd unlock the kitchen door and pocket the key.

Tonight, when Mum thought he was safely in his room, he'd come back.

That evening Nathan joined Grandpa in the hotel lobby.

"Hi, Gramp. Mum's ringing the owner of the cottage."

"So she said." Grandpa patted the sofa. "Sit next to me, Nathaniel. So you found somewhere to live, eh?" He smiled lopsidedly, his eyes approving. "That didn't take you long."

Nathan grinned. "Mum says it's beginner's luck."

"Reckon you deserve some. You've had a rough time lately, what with Max and all."

"I do miss him, Gramp. We did a lot together. Swimming. Homework. Played the piano. Made breakfast every morning while Mum was in the bath. I can't get used to the gap."

Grandpa clanked his sherry glass on the table. "I know. Funny, I was thinking the same kind of thing only this afternoon."

"You were?"

"My Christmas tree. I was putting up the decorations. It's the first time I've done that since Grandma died. I couldn't face it last year, went to my friend Charlie's for Christmas lunch. But now that you and your mum are here, I wanted to make an effort. I mean, you two *and* Charlie will be coming to me for Christmas this year."

"Thanks, Gramp."

"My pleasure. At least, it was until I was standing there with all the lights fixed and just about to turn them on. Suddenly I heard Grandma's voice in my head saying, 'That looks lovely, Henry. Best ever.' And tears started pouring down my face like she'd left me only yesterday."

Nathan reached out and took Grandpa's surprisingly cold and bony hand. "Tomorrow *I'll* come and tell you the tree looks great. Then you can hear *my* voice."

Grandpa gave a shaky laugh. "You're a good boy, Nathaniel. That's a very nice thought." The last drops of sherry slid past the moustache. "Ah, here she is."

Mum joined them, sitting down and lighting a cigarette.

"I do wish you wouldn't, Elizabeth."

"Dad! Give me a break!"

"Well?" Nathan swallowed. "Did you speak to Mr Croft?"

"Yes." She inhaled. "I rather wish I hadn't. Someone else is interested. Nothing's signed and sealed, but they're negotiating. I'm afraid we've missed the boat."

Nathan stared at her. "That's impossible."

"We're too late and there's an end to it. Mr Croft was

most abrupt. In fact he was quite rude. I'm not bothering with him again."

"Wait a minute." Grandpa leaned towards her. "Did you say Croft? Is his name *Jake* Croft?"

"Yes," Nathan said impatiently. "Why, do you know him?"

Grandpa hesitated. "The name rings a bell. When I ran the local paper, I used to know everyone ... But there was something nasty in the woodshed about Jake Croft. Very nasty." He clenched his fist and drummed it against his forehead. "Damned if I can remember precisely what."

"Well, he was certainly nasty to me. Anyone would think it was me trying to sell him something he didn't want! And I agreed to the asking price."

"We can't give up just like that." Nathan's mouth tasted of grit. He wanted to run back to the cottage, crash at the door, demand to be heard. "We must sort it out, talk to him again." He looked to Grandpa for support. "Offer him more money. Anything."

"Don't be silly, Nathan." Mum stubbed out the cigarette. She looked suddenly exhausted. "I knew it had all happened too easily. Things don't fall into your lap like that. There's always a catch."

Fury gripped Nathan. It made him cruel. "If we can't buy that cottage, I won't live down here. I'll stay in London with Dad. With Tom. With anyone who'll have me."

"Hang on a minute." Grandpa shot Mum a worried smile. "That's blackmail. You can't say things like that. There'll be other places."

"Of course there will." Mum's eyes sparked with tears. "We've only *started* looking. There's bound to be somewhere else. Maybe somewhere better."

"No, there won't." Nathan stood up. "You don't understand. There's something special about that cottage. And the garden and the cat and  –" He backed away from them. "I don't want any supper. Couldn't eat a thing."

Mum reached up to grab his hand. "We must keep our heads. We can't get carried away like this."

"Carried away?" He wrenched his hand out of hers. "How can you *say* that?" His cheeks burned. "I wish I'd never *found* the place! Never told you about it." He glared at the two startled faces in front of him. "The one time I manage to sort things, make you listen to me, and what happens? It all goes wrong because *you've* screwed things up."

He turned away, ran through the lobby, down the corridor, into his room. He threw himself on the bed.

*I can't believe this is happening. Just when I thought things might work out ... If I don't sort this, I might never see Rosalie again. I'm going back to the cottage tonight. As soon as the coast is clear.*

* * *

Mum came to check on him. Nathan did not look up. She said, "Sulking won't get you anywhere. Not ever. See you in the morning." She slammed the door.

A waiter brought him chicken pie with chips and a lumpy banana sponge. Nathan chomped through them. If talking to Mum didn't make any difference and shutting up was equally useless, there had to be *something* he could do to be heard. She listened to the people she worked with, didn't she? She read the stupid letters from all her adoring fans ... Thought about them ... Took them seriously ... Answered them ...

He got up and scrabbled in his bag for some paper and a pen. His hand shook with anger and haste as he wrote:

*Dear Lizzie*

*My parents have split up and now my mum wants to take me away from our home and move miles away. She says she's trying to get her life sorted, but what about mine? She never thinks about what I want, and she won't listen to a word I say. What should I do?*

*Yours sincerely*
*Benjamin Smith*

He found an envelope in a drawer and wrote *To Lizzie Fielding* on it, then sealed it and dashed out of his room, along the corridor to the foyer. At the reception desk, he said, "This is for Mrs Fielding. For tomorrow morning." The girl behind the desk was dealing with other guests and hardly glanced at him. She put the envelope into the rack behind her.

Back in his room, he hunched in a chair and stared blankly at the TV. Writing that letter hadn't made him feel any better. If anything, it made him feel worse. Breakfast would probably be a nightmare. As if he cared ...

At ten o'clock, with a sigh of relief, he flicked off the screen. He pulled on his boots and coat, opened the window, slid out and left it ajar.

A cool wind sighed in the fir trees under a full silver-sharp moon. He turned towards the path through the woods. It was darker and longer, but the one through the golf course was also the route for cars. Grandpa would be on his way home from supper. *I don't want him spotting me in his headlights like a frightened rabbit.*

The damp, slippery path made running impossible. An owl hooted above him, mournful, menacing. It plunged close to the stream, hovered, pounced with a splash of water. There was a short, high yelp of pain. *That sounds like Rosalie's laugh.* Victorious over its prey, the bird swooped into the trees.

The moon vanished behind clouds. An eerie quiet gripped the woods. Nathan's heart thudded. Bushes loomed in weird clusters. Surely the path was longer? It was certainly less familiar.

He looked up, praying for the moon's light. Even the branches above him seemed to spin and weave, as if they were setting him some impossible convoluted puzzle. Then he saw the iron gate and through it the road. He caught his breath with relief.

He began to jog along the streets. Windows threw spangles of glowing light, their curtains open. He could see their rooms, the shambles of bottles, glasses and candles, the Christmas trees dangling with bulbs. A front door opened as he passed and a buzz of voices gusted out. He gazed enviously at the guests on the doorstep and wished he could join them.

At the top of the cul-de-sac he stopped and almost ran away. The street looked so quiet and scary. What if Jake Croft was in the cottage? What was the point of *asking* for trouble?

But Rosalie might need him. He might just be able to

help. He'd got this far, it seemed daft to give up now. He felt in his jeans' pocket. The key to the kitchen door warmed beneath his touch.

His courage returned and he pressed on.

Dark and silent, the cottage stood waiting for him. Curtains were drawn across the attic window. It looked like a black-zipped mouth, refusing to reveal its secrets. Nathan slipped down the side of the cottage to the kitchen door.

He tried the handle. The door stuck, squeaked and then relented.

He stood inside, his heart racing. Gradually his eyes made sense of the dark shapes of the kitchen. He stripped off his coat, kicked off his boots and left them on the floor.

He listened in the darkness.

Not a sound.

He tiptoed through the kitchen, into the hall, up the first flight of stairs. On the second he skidded on the dusty pine. He gripped the banister, willing himself to climb.

A sound throbbed into the darkness. He stood behind the attic door listening to a voice, half-singing, half-chanting, high and like a bell:

*Candle shining in the night with your enchanted flame*
*By the powers of magic might, listen to my name*
*As you shed your light, your gleam, at this mystic hour*
*May fulfilment of my dream harvest secret power*
*Flame of magic, blue and gold, turn the wheel of fortune bold*
*Flame of magic, ice and fire, grant me this my one desire.*

Nathan waited in the swirl of silence that followed. The song seemed to echo and resound in his head. Then he plucked up courage and pushed at the door.

Moonlight from the back-garden window flooded the attic with an intense silvery light. The air tasted thick with the scent of incense: a potent, heady mixture of sandlewood and cedar.

The girl knelt in the centre of the room. Around her burned clutches of small candles. They cast leaping shadows on the walls, flickered their light on to her face, made a halo of her hair.

She looked up, startled, and scrambled to her feet. "Nathan?"

"Yes." He stumbled into the attic.

"Shit, you gave me a fright!"

"Sorry. I didn't mean to scare you."

"Well, you bloody well did!" Her voice shook. "Make a habit of this, do you?"

"What do you mean?"

"Wandering around St Ives at night, walking into people's houses –"

"'Course not."

"So why on *earth* are you here?"

"I had to see you ..." His eyes got used to the flickering shadows. He gazed at her. She wore a long cream linen tunic with wide sleeves. It made her look older, thinner, more frail – almost ghostly.

"In the middle of the night? How the hell did you get in?"

He was suddenly reminded of Jake Croft in the garden, demanding, "Who the hell are you?" He'd been frightened then, but now if anything he was even more scared. The attic looked so different. He'd scarcely have recognised Rosalie. This was like being in a different world.

He said hastily, his mouth dry, "This morning. I unlocked the kitchen door before we left. I've got the key."

Stiffly, he held it out to her.

"You're an idiot." She moved towards him and snatched it from his hand. The tips of her fingers felt icy cold. "You don't want to get mixed up in my life."

He noticed the thin shine of tears on her cheeks. "Yes, I do. I already am." He looked down at the candles, how they clustered in a semicircle on the floor. "What's with all this?"

"What does it look like?"

"I don't know." He hesitated. The lights from the flames seemed to flutter beneath his eyelids, made him flinch and blink. "I read a book once. On witchcraft ... Just now ... Were you chanting a spell or something?"

"How long had you been listening at the door?"

"Not long ... You make it sound as if I've been spying on you!"

"Well, haven't you?"

"No." Nathan was relieved the darkness hid his blushes. "Yes. I mean, I'm sorry that's what it feels like. I never meant –"

"And I suppose now you think I'm a mad witch who's stirring up sickly potions and putting spells on people!"

"I don't think anything of the sort!"

"Good!" She pushed back her hair, her voice defiant. "I was praying, if you must know. Praying to Mum that nobody will buy this cottage. That her spirit will allow me to stay. That anybody who might want it will find something better. Much better."

"Including me?"

Rosalie's eyes burned into his. "I can make magic things happen, you know. I didn't tell you that, did I? I can still hear Mum's voice. Here, in this room. When I'm painting, she talks to me. She and I still work together."

"Do you?" Nathan suddenly remembered his last conversation with Mum and what he'd come to tell Rosalie. He moved towards her, grasped her arm, felt its thinness beneath the tunic. "Then magic this away. Mum rang your dad about the cottage because we wanted to buy it. But he said someone else has already made an offer."

The girl swayed on her feet. "I don't believe you."

"It's the truth."

"This is happening so fast I can't breathe." She grabbed his hand. "Will you pray with me?" There was a wildness about her now, a new urgency in her voice.

"How?" Prickles of alarm shot through him. "Who to?"

She pulled him into the semicircle of candles. "Kneel with me ... Put your hands like this ... Now close your eyes and pray that nobody will buy this cottage."

"Out loud?"

"No. In silence. But pray really hard. Shout the words in your head as if you were trying to make them travel for miles and miles over rivers and mountains."

Nathan dropped his head and closed his eyes. The warmth of the candles fanned more gently now against his eyelids.

*I don't want anyone to buy this cottage – but if anyone does, let it be Mum and me. So Rosalie won't have lost it completely. Please let something good come out of all this mess, this moving away from everything I love. Please.*

He opened his eyes.

The girl was looking at him, her face strange, questioning. "Did you pray?"

"Yes." He sat back on his heels. "Do you think it'll work?"

"I hope so. But I can never tell. It takes time. You have to go on praying."

"I don't get all this. Why *is* your dad selling this place? If it means so much to you, surely he could –"

"He hasn't got a job." She looked defeated. "He hasn't had a proper one since ... not for a long time. Mum left him some money, but he's used it all up. He's on the dole, but he's got debts. They get bigger all the time. He does odd jobs for people, but the minute they give him cash he spends it on booze. He can't afford to keep the cottage and he's got nothing else to sell."

"I'm sorry. My dad – he's –"

"Is he down here with you?"

"No." Nathan took a deep breath. "He left us in September. Found himself a new family."

"Oh." She stared down at the candles. "So you know what it's like."

"Yes. Sometimes a whole day goes by and I manage to get through it without remembering." Talking about it to her, he felt tears burning his eyes. "Then something happens to remind me he's not there. That he's never going to be there. He doesn't *belong* to me any more." He tried to calm the wobble in his voice. "He says he wants me to be a part of his new family, but I know that's not true. They come first now, not me."

"At least your dad's alive. You can still see him, even if it isn't all the time." She brushed at her face with her long fingers. "Dead people only live in your head. In what you imagine, what you dream. It's so hard –"

The moonlight from the window vanished behind a cloud. In the sudden darkening of the room the girl raised her head. "Someone's coming."

Nathan scrambled to his feet. "How do you know?"

"I can feel it ... I can't explain ... You must go."

"Will you be OK?"

A faint smile lit her face. She stood up and touched his shoulder. "Yes, boy in the garden. I can look after myself ...

Hurry, before you get caught."

Nathan stood in the dark kitchen, pulling on his boots and coat. His legs shook with haste. Something stirred in a corner the other side of the room. A pair of yellow eyes, suddenly alert, met his.

"Tiggy?" Nathan moved towards her, bent to stroke the fur, warm with sleep. But she was wide awake now, listening, her body taut.

Nathan froze. He heard the splutter of a van, a screech of brakes, a door slam. The front door opened.

"Ros?" Footsteps plodded into the hall.

*Shit. Don't let him come into the kitchen. Please.*

"Ros? Are you up there?" Jake Croft's voice thundered through the cottage. "We've got a buyer. We've got to clear up all our stuff, fast. Come and give me a hand with these chairs."

Nathan made a dive for the kitchen door. He wrenched it open and slid through. He closed it behind him as quietly as his shaking hands would allow. He flattened his body against the wall.

Through the window in the door he saw lights flick on in the hall, then in the kitchen. Again the voice rang out.

"Will you come and make yourself *useful* for a change?"

There was no reply.

Furniture scraped across the floor, banged against the walls. Jake Croft swore. The van doors opened and slammed. More tramping.

"Thanks for nothing, girl!"

The lights flicked out and the front door shut. Footsteps tramped down the path. The engine revved and the van lurched away.

Nathan waited in the silence, his ribs aching with the thump of his heart.

*That was close!*

He slipped back into the kitchen.

*I must check that Rosalie's OK.*

He raced up the stairs to the attic, pushed abruptly at the door and stood in a sea of moonlight. The candles had been blown out. Thin plumes of feathery smoke fanned upwards towards the moon, like pale moths trying to escape.

"Rosalie?"

In the stillness that met his voice Nathan knew the attic was empty. He stood over the desk, turned on its small lamp. The painting of the two shadowy people on the beach had gone. He moved towards the window, pressed his hands against the curtains, knowing even as he did so that Rosalie was not behind them.

He switched off the lamp. The moonlight seemed to crush against his shoulder. For a moment he looked out at the garden, the shivering grass, the moonlit branches swaying in the wind, the high clouds chasing across the sky.

Behind him he heard the faintest chink of bottles.

He spun round. The smell of salt and tar seemed to fill the attic. He heard other sounds: laughter, the faintest of voices. More clinking. He looked out to the garden, thinking they must have come from there, then back to the attic, and gasped.

In the semicircle of candles stood three shapes, almost like bodies, transparent as moths' wings, their arms hovering around each other. A old man and a woman, but he couldn't make out their faces, and another much younger woman with flowing curly hair.

Nathan blinked. The shapes began to circle round and round in perfect harmony, as if they were dancing to the beat of a drum or the cry of a violin, their heads flung back in delighted silent laughter.

The circling grew faster and they began to spin. The shapes became a single whirling spiral of light.

Then they slowed, stopped, separated, climbed the arc of moonlight – and vanished through the window into the garden and the dark shimmer of sky.

Nathan's legs gave out beneath him. He sat at the desk, trembling, too frightened to move, to look round again. He spread his arms over the wood, comforted by its warmth, laid his head down. Covered in moonlight, he seemed to sleep.

He woke, minutes later, deeply refreshed, as if he had been swept out to sea, dived into its utmost depths, reached into the centre of his own being.

He stood up, looked down at his feet, at the attic floor. He stooped to touch one of the candles. The wax at its base was still warm. He could smell the sharp, invigorating cleanness of its burnt wick.

And then he noticed.

The candle at the tip of the semicircle had vanished. So wherever Rosalie had gone, she had taken it with her.

Nathan stumbled back to Tregenna along darker streets. The parties were over, their guests gone, the curtains drawn, the lights out. Empty beer cans rattled in the gutter.

But the woods, more alive than ever, crawled with secret mutterings. The wind sang in his ears, colder, insistently. Clouds swept across the sky, blotting and releasing the moon. A wild cat, growling, shot in front of him, vanished into the thicket.

He reached the hotel, climbed through his window and crashed exhausted on to the bed. Strange, muddled dreams swelled his mind: of terror in the woods, the shrieking owl, Rosalie's chanting, the candlelight, her halo of bright hair. A moth-like apparition spun before his eyes, laughing as it twirled.

He woke with a start, his body drenched in sweat, the smell of salt and tar in his nostrils.

"You look tired," Mum said frostily as he stomped towards their breakfast table. "Didn't you sleep well?"

"No." He slumped into a chair.

"If it's any consolation, neither did I." She rustled her newspaper. "I suppose you think this 'Benjamin Smith' letter" – it was lying beneath her plate –"is a way of getting me to change my mind about moving. I have to say I'm very unimpressed."

"You take your readers seriously." Nathan felt the old anger begin to bubble in his stomach. "Why can't you listen to *me*?"

"I *do* listen to you. You're the absolute fixed-point centre of my life. You know that in your heart, but you just don't want to admit it. I care more about you than all my readers put together." Her hand shook as she poured her tea. "But they're grateful to me for my help. You should see some of the thank-you letters I get. I can change people's lives with a bit of sympathy and understanding. And I want that to continue. It's *got* to continue, it's my career and our livelihood. So don't make a mockery of it by pretending that people write to me as a silly joke."

Nathan didn't answer. He wolfed his way through an enormous breakfast while Mum watched him, drank tea and messed about with a piece of toast. Eventually she said, "What are your plans for today?"

He avoided her eyes. "I'm going to Gramp's. I saw some paints in the art shop on the waterfront. I thought he could buy me some for Christmas."

"Well, it'll be nice of him if he does." She folded her serviette. "Perhaps you'll have the grace to apologise for your behaviour last night. I was thoroughly ashamed of you."

"Sorry."

"You hide away in your room, sulking like a three-year-old. You're nearly fourteen, for God's sake. Why don't you grow up and act your age?"

"Don't go *on* about it."

She pushed back her chair. "I'm going to Waterberry's Estate Agents. Would you like to come?"

Nathan stared at the marmalade. "No, thanks."

"Right. Look, Nathan, I need to make one thing clear."

"What?" With an effort he met her eyes.

"You're moving down here with me, whatever we buy and wherever we find it. Of course, I want you to *like* the place. But I *will* not have you kicking up at every opportunity like a spoilt brat."

He scowled. "I'm not a –"

"Then don't behave like one. I've done my best to see your point of view. It's high time you saw mine." She gathered her bag, the letter, her papers. "I'll see you for lunch in Kathy's Bar. One o'clock. And *don't* be late."

She brushed past.

Nathan flicked at crumbs until they spattered the carpet.

*That's all I need. A lecture over scrambled eggs. After the night I've had. What does she know?*

He stood up and slouched over to a window. Two men were packing bags into their car, checking some papers, zipping up their jackets. He watched them but he thought about something else.

He thought about Jake Croft. About something Grandpa had said. Something nasty he hadn't quite remembered. Maybe if he said sorry, got him talking, he could jog his memory. Maybe if he managed to get to the bottom of what was wrong with Jake Croft, he could go back to Rosalie and help her properly. It was worth a try.

And he had nothing better to do.

Grandpa opened the door. "Nathaniel! Lovely surprise. And good timing. Just baked some scones. Would you like one?"

"You bet." He followed Grandpa across the hall, paused at the living-room door. "Gramp! The tree's fantastic!"

"I turned on its lights when I got home last night and it looked an absolute treat." He pulled out a kitchen stool.

"Sit yourself down." He sliced into a piping-hot scone. "Have this with blackberry jam."

Nathan took a deep breath. "Sorry about yesterday. I was just so angry –"

"Apology accepted." Grandpa rattled a cup and saucer at the sink. "I know how you feel –"

"Do you? It's not just any old cottage, Gramp. It's special because I found it and I thought I was getting things sorted –"

"I know you did. But you can't wave a magic wand and expect a fairy godmother to come jumping out of the hedgerow. Sometimes things don't work out the way you planned. You must stop feeling sorry for yourself."

"I'm *not*, Gramp –"

"You have been. Life's tough. You win some, you lose some. You can't spend it wishing things hadn't happened."

"But everything's so *unfair* –"

"Look." Grandpa reached for a cloth. "When your Grandma died, I could've gone to pieces. I didn't. I picked myself up and dug the garden for three days, sobbing my heart out. Then I taught myself to run the house like a battleship. I learned to cook, got out, saw friends. I go to my old newspaper office every week, catch up with the gossip, read the latest copy. I walk in all weathers, sing in the church choir ... Get it?"

"It's *different* for you, Gramp."

"Claptrap. It's exactly the same. Grandma lives in me all the time, every minute. I love her to bits, always have. But I've got to get *on* with life, like she would've done. Moping, whining, making other people's lives a misery won't get you anywhere."

Nathan looked at his plate. "It's not just that Dad's left. It's my best friend Tom and me. We've always been together. Now Mum's going to split *us* up as well."

"Friends can't *be* split up," Grandpa said swiftly. "Not if you *want* to keep in touch. Phone, write, send an email. All this high-tech stuff makes it so easy. You can see each other in the holidays. Love never dies – as long as you keep it alive."

Nathan chewed the last of the scone, licked the jam off his fingers. "Gramp, last night, when we were talking about the cottage."

"Yes?"

"You said something about Jake Croft. Have you remembered anything?"

"Damned if I have." Grandpa sat down at the table, his bony hands round a mug of coffee. "My memory's not what it used to be. It must have been a fair while ago."

"*How* long?"

Grandpa shook his head. "No idea." He frowned. "Quite a time."

"And when you ran the paper, would you have written about it?"

"Well, *I* wouldn't, because I was the editor of the whole thing. But yes, one of my reporters would have been on the case."

"So if I wanted to find out about Jake Croft," Nathan persevered, "I'd need to track down a copy of the article."

"I suppose you would." Grandpa looked at him doubtfully. "Why are you so interested?"

Nathan flushed. "The day after I found the cottage, I went back to write down the 'for sale' number. I bumped into Jake Croft in the garden. He nearly beat me up."

"*Did* he indeed!" Anger flashed in Grandpa's eyes. "And how is finding out about him going to help?"

"It just is," Nathan said firmly. "Call it unfinished business." He rushed on. "At school we're doing this project on local news and how you can research it. I thought I could kind of combine the two."

Grandpa hesitated. Then he said, "I'll let you into a secret. Guess what's lurking in my attic."

"What?"

"Thirty years' worth of my newspaper."

"Gramp! You're joking!"

"I'm deadly serious. Every so often Grandma would threaten a clear-out. I'd rush up and tidy the *St Ives Recorder* into their proper years, dust them, arrange them in their box files. I never let her throw them away."

"You mean I could look through them?"

"I reckon you could." Grandpa gave his lopsided smile. "So! The Henry Gorst Archive will finally serve its purpose! ... There's just one thing, though." He touched Nathan's shoulder. "I hope you like spiders."

"Good grief!" Grandpa said. They had climbed the rope ladder into the attic and stood blinking in the half-light. "It's even more of a mess than I remembered ... Mind you, I don't suppose I've tidied anything away since Grandma died."

Nathan picked cobwebs from his hair. "Can I look at the *Recorder* up here?"

Grandpa ran his hand along one of the walls, found a switch and turned on a naked overhead light. "It'll be a lot quicker than carting the files up and down that rope ladder!" He moved over to a corner. "The collection starts here, on the left-hand side. But you won't need to check any of that until at least here." He dragged a large green box file from a shelf. "Why don't you start with this?" He dumped the file on the floor.

A cloud of dust swirled into Nathan's eyes. "Right." A steely determination filled him. "Thanks, Gramp. Leave me to it."

"Let battle commence." Grandpa disappeared down the ladder. White wisps of hair bobbed for a moment from the floor. "If you need me, stick your head out and yell."

*"Right, Nat."*

Nathan heard Dad's voice.

*"A lesson in research. Don't just plunge in and muddle through. Think it out. Look at one whole newspaper and work out its format. You'll find the interesting articles in the front, with stuff like letters and editorials in the middle, and sport and all the ads at the back.*

*"If Jake Croft was a bad boy and got into big trouble – enough for Grandpa to remember something nasty – then it'll probably have made headlines. Not necessarily front-page news, but something meaty on pages two or three."*

Nathan knelt on the floor, opened the box and pulled out the first newspaper.

*"And don't read anything properly. It's tempting to get involved with the items of news. Just skim-read the headlines, fast as you can.*

*Look for the name Croft and nothing else. Keep going."*

January. The headlines described vile weather, a storm at sea, the stalwart work of the RNLI, a wrecked ship, lost lives. Mourners stood by the shore as rain poured down on them, their tears at one with the elements.

He flicked the paper open and scoured its format. Yes: he could limit himself to the first couple of pages – at least the first time round.

An hour later he'd checked twelve box files and was none the wiser. His back ached, his shoulders throbbed, his knees were sore, his hands grimy with newsprint. He closed his eyes. Black letters sparked in his head. He stared around the attic.

*Nothing, Dad. Not a shred. I'll have to go back over my tracks. Either check everything again or start a year earlier.*

*"Stick with it, Nat. Patience usually pays off in the end. Where will you start this time?"*

Nathan craned his neck at the sagging shelves. *I'll go back a shelf. I may have to try again tomorrow. I've got to meet Mum at one o'clock and before that I want to go to the art shop with Grandpa.*

He stood up, stretched his back and shoulders, flexed inky fingers, brushed the dust off his jeans. He dragged another two box files from the shelf.

*Come on, Mr Croft. I know you're in here somewhere.*

Ten minutes later, Nathan found Jake Croft. He'd made front-page headlines after all. The photograph startled him: Croft's face, younger, more powerful. His smile, threatening, almost malicious, leered from the page. He wore no hat this time: his straight dark hair fell in thick strands over his forehead.

*I've found him, Dad!*

*"Congratulations, Nat! What does the article say?"*

Nathan blinked as the words danced in front of his eyes: the headlines he'd hoped for and yet, somehow, the news he'd been dreading to find. His hands started to sweat. He sat back on his heels, clutched the faded yellow paper to his chest.

*Please God, don't let them mention Rosalie.*

He began to read:

## OWNER OF CROFT'S YARD ARRESTED

*Mr Jake Croft, the owner of Croft's Yard, was charged yesterday morning with receiving stolen goods. Customs officials, who swooped in a dawn raid on the yard, found a large haul of expensive French wines and tobacco in a boat Mr Croft had been repairing for a* client. *Mr Croft has refused to reveal his client's name.*

*Mr Croft has protested his innocence. He claimed that an old acquaintance had a grudge against him and had planted the goods. He said he could not be held responsible.*

*Croft's Yard, which has been in Mr Croft's family for several generations, will be closed until further notice.*

*Mr Croft's wife, Moira, a well-known Cornish painter, who has a ten-year-old daughter, said she was devastated by the news. "I shall fight every step of the way for my husband's release. He would never get mixed up in petty smuggling. Croft's Yard has always had an impeccable reputation. There has been some terrible mistake."*

Nathan slammed the paper shut, threw it into its box and dragged the files back to their shelves. His mouth tasted of ink.

He stared down at his feet, where a clutch of more recent newspapers sat waiting to be filed. Automatically, he gathered up a bundle and shoved them on a shelf, coughing at the swirls of dust. He bent again for a second pile – and stopped.

Staring up at him was a photo of a woman so like Rosalie it made the breath catch in his lungs. She had the same slender face, the cloud of pale hair.

Nathan shivered. *Those whirling shapes I saw last night – the younger one. That was Moira Croft ... So I did see ghosts ... I can't wait to tell Rosalie ...*

He crouched over the paper.

## LOCAL ARTIST FOUND DEAD IN MYSTERIOUS CLIFF FALL

*Moira Croft, a well-known local artist, was found dead yesterday morning on the cliff plateau at the bottom of her garden. Her twelve-year-old daughter, Rosalie, is said to have found her, although the exact circumstances are still unclear.*

*Mrs Croft's husband, Jake Croft, formerly of Croft's Yard, is currently in France. Every effort is being made to trace him and bring him home.*

*Moira Croft will be much missed. She lived all her life in St Ives and established an excellent reputation, both here and abroad. A small exhibition of her work was held at the Tate St Ives gallery last year.*

*A full obituary will appear on Friday.*

Nathan picked up the paper and squashed it into the pile on the shelf. He'd found more than he'd been looking for, he thought bitterly. He'd tell Grandpa about Croft's Yard – but he'd keep the stuff about Moira Croft to himself ...

"Any luck?" Grandpa was stirring a pot on the stove.

"You could say that."

Grandpa looked at him. "Heavens, boy, you're filthy."

Nathan slumped on to a kitchen stool. "Ever heard of Croft's Boat Yard?"

"Of course! *Now* I remember!" Grandpa handed him a wet flannel. "Here, wipe your face ... Famous yard, traded on the coast for donkey's years. Jake Croft inherited it when his father died. Not a bad little business, but Croft got involved with some shady dealings, became greedy, blew the lot. The police closed the yard down. Lots of people lost a lot of money. Big money. It costs a great deal these days to build even the smallest boat."

"You mean Croft was guilty?"

"Seems like it. They made him a bankrupt. He got eighteen months in jail if my memory serves me right."

Nathan looked up at him. The dust of the attic, the taste of ink and now the heat of the wet flannel made his stomach churn. "What happened to the yard?"

"Someone else bought it at a fraction of its worth. Got it up and running again in a couple of weeks."

"Could Croft have been framed?"

"Who knows, Nathaniel? When guys like him get in the deep end, who knows where the truth begins and ends?" He grinned. "I'm the last person to ask. I used to run a newspaper ... By the way." He turned back to the stove and switched it off. "It's probably a good thing you won't be buying Croft's cottage."

"Why?" Nathan did his best to sound unconcerned.

"I reckon he could be pretty dangerous. If you want my advice, you'll stay well away from him."

9

In the art shop, Grandpa introduced him. "Charlie, this is my grandson. I call him Nathaniel but to everyone else, he's Nathan."

Charlie gave a guffaw of approval. "Hi, Nathan." That deep burr again. "Weren't you here yesterday?"

"Well spotted." Nathan looked at Charlie's lean, narrow face, untidy grey curls, generous mouth, smiling deep-blue eyes. He shook a roughened hand. "But yesterday I was just looking."

"And now?"

"Gramp's buying me a Christmas present."

"I'm delighted to hear it." Charlie waved an arm. "Masses to choose from. Take your pick."

"Charlie's one of my oldest friends," Grandpa said. "Cornwall born and bred, trained at an art college in London, came back here to live as a fully-fledged cartoonist. You've worked for the *St Ives Recorder* for how long now, Charlie?"

"Almost twenty-five years, for my sins. Your grandfather, Nathan, saved my bacon and no mistake." Charlie and

Grandpa grinned at each other. "I'd never have been able to buy this place and open this shop without the money I make on the *Recorder*. There's a marvellous studio at the back, where I can draw to my heart's content, and a flat above where I sleep. All this thanks to Henry."

"Oh, come on, Charlie." Grandpa beamed with delight. "If I hadn't spotted a talent like yours, someone else would've. Right, to business, Nathaniel. Get browsing."

Nathan chose a set of coloured pencils, watercolours, brushes and silky art paper. Charlie wrapped them and Grandpa tucked them under his arm.

"See you tonight, Henry?" Charlie said. "At Carols by Candlelight?"

"Haven't missed it in thirty years." Grandpa looked at Nathan. "Will you and your mum come? I'm in the choir. We make a wonderful racket. Well worth hearing."

"I'd love to," Nathan said, but his head buzzed with worries. "I'll tell Mum."

They left the shop and stood looking out at the waterfront.

"Thanks, Gramp. For lending me your archive. For the Christmas present."

"My pleasure. It's the first time we've really talked, man to man. It's been a good morning."

"Yes."

Nathan stared across at a group of men standing by the boats. They talked, argued, dipped their heads over cigarettes. The smoke spiralled into the midday air in thin white funnels above their boisterous voices.

One of the men drew away, tall, heavy, his dark green hat pulled down over his eyes. He shouted something at the group, made a rude gesture and began to stride up towards the shops.

The group snarled at his back and closed ranks behind him.

"What's the matter?" Grandpa gripped Nathan's arm.

"It's nothing. Nothing at all."

"You've got a face like thunder. Was it something I said?"

"'Course not, Gramp. You've been brilliant."

Grandpa's grip slackened. "See you tonight, then. Pick me up at seven."

Nathan backed into a doorway. He watched as Jake Croft pulled at his cigarette and with a swift, practised gesture, flung the butt into the thin grey sludge of tide.

Nathan began to walk away across the waterfront, but something made him stop in his tracks and turn. He saw Jake slouch past the art shop as Charlie came out of it. For a moment the two men glared at each other, face to face, their shoulders squared like threatening boxers. Then, silently, abruptly, Jake brushed away.

Charlie stared after him, his fists clenched. He turned to inspect the window, his body taut, his face black with anger. He crashed back into the shop.

Nathan ran to find out what was new in the window.

At the centre of the display stood a painting, framed in pale wood. A painting he recognised: two shadowy people on a beach pushed against the wind, the sky behind them dark with thunderclouds. Underneath it sat a label:

*Figures on a Beach*
*New work by young local artist Rosalie Croft*

Nathan drank his soup as fast as he could while Mum went on about the houses she'd seen. "But none of them are right. I'll soldier on while I've got the energy. I'm inspecting two more cottages this afternoon. I'll meet you back at Tregenna. We can have supper there before the carol concert."

He watched her scurrying down the hill, the sheaf of papers under her arm. A moment later, he followed. He was going to the cottage, but this time bold as brass.

* * *

As he reached it, he saw a new notice on the wooden post:

*Sold. No Further Calls or Callers.*

He wanted to rip the piece of paper from its nail and tear it into shreds.

He flung open the gate, marched up the path and drilled his thumb against the doorbell. He hopped from foot to foot and rang again. He heard steps on the stairs.

"Who is it?"

"It's Nathan. Let me in."

She opened the door, her face smeared with dust. She didn't bother with a greeting. "I'm clearing out the attic." She blushed. "I must look a mess."

He stepped into the hall. "You look great ... So does your painting. I saw it in Charlie's window."

"I managed to finish it. I've tried so many times to get it right but it never worked before. Yesterday afternoon, it suddenly all came together. I couldn't believe it."

"Where were you last night? After your dad left? I came to find you –"

She avoided his eyes. "I jumped on to my broomstick and flew out of the window."

"My ghosts did too ... Fly out of the window, that is."

Relief swept through him that at last he could tell her.

"*What?*"

"I saw three ghosts ... It was so weird. I thought I heard the chink of bottles and there was a funny smell, salty ... and black, like tar. Then I saw shapes, almost like bodies, but transparent ... An old couple with a younger woman –"

Rosalie's face changed. A new interest and respect lit her eyes. "What were they doing?"

"Laughing, spinning in each other's arms ... It was only for a moment. I thought I must be dreaming, thought I saw them climb the moonbeam through the window ... And then I passed out, I was so scared. I don't know what happened next. I guess I must have fallen asleep."

Her face was pale. "I'm glad."

"Why?"

"That you've seen them too."

"Who *are* they?"

"My grandparents ... my father's mum and dad."

"And the woman?" He moved closer towards her. "Is she your mum?"

"Yes."

"I've just read about her in the *St Ives Recorder*. And about your dad. At least ... a bit about him. About the yard."

"How did you –?"

"My grandpa's got a collection of the newspapers in his attic. He used to be the editor. He let me search through them. I found the headlines and the photographs."

She pushed back her hair with a grimy hand. "And you want to know the whole story?"

"If you want to tell me."

"OK, you win!" She paused, smiled faintly. "Cup of tea, Sherlock Holmes?"

The kitchen table groaned with stacks of cups and plates. Cupboard doors stood open, a basket of crumpled washing spilled over in a corner. Tiggy slept profoundly in a nest of pillowcases, her paws looped over her eyes.

He watched Rosalie move about the room, washing her hands, filling the kettle, picking out two mugs, dropping teabags into the pot.

"It's not a nice story, I warn you." She poured boiling water. "It was four years ago. I was ten when everything fell apart." She put the pot on the table and sat facing him, her eyes fixed on memories. "Dad ran the boat yard, Mum painted pictures. Wonderful landscapes, people's portraits –"

"Like the one in the hall?"

"Yes. Charlie bought everything Mum painted. He was wonderful to us when –". she faltered.

"Your dad went to prison?"

Her voice darkened. "Charlie was one of the few people in St Ives who stood by us. Even my best friend, Bella – she lives at the top of this road – even she gave me the cold shoulder and we've never really been close since.

"And at school it was ghastly. The teachers were oh-so-polite, but when I walked into a classroom, everything used to go quiet and I knew they'd been talking about me ... about Dad."

"So how did it all start?"

"Dad had worked in the boat yard ever since he left school. *His* dad owned the yard and he trained him up. Then he died and Dad took over ... When Mum got pregnant with me, she said it was the best surprise she'd ever had. But Dad – he'd always wanted a son." Unsteadily she poured the tea. "Mum said he went out and got drunk!"

"Did he often do that?"

"No. He was a big, jolly man, always laughing, joking with the guys in the yard. I used to love being with him. He worked hard, knew everyone for miles around. He adored Mum. He was never a crook ... or a smuggler."

She pushed his mug of tea across the table, raised her own and smiled at him. "May you never thirst. That's what

Mum used to say to the special people in her life."

His cheeks burnt with sudden joy. "Cheers." He gulped at the hot liquid. "So what happened?"

She dropped her gaze. "It was October, four years ago. I got home from school, Mum was crying. Dad had been arrested. She'd no idea why. Then everything became a nightmare – reporters on the doorstep, people ringing up. All I knew was Dad had been taken away from us. They locked him up and he didn't come home for eighteen months."

"Did he tell you his side of the story?"

"The more Mum asked, the more he clammed up. He just said he was innocent, over and over again and refused to tell us anything."

"Do *you* think he was guilty?"

She looked at him. "I don't know. I'll probably never know." She bit her lip. "Him being in prison was bad enough. But Mum and I made a life for ourselves. When he got home, things were worse. He had no job, nobody would give him work, his friends blanked him, he got very depressed."

"How did you manage?"

"Mum went on painting, day and night. Dad began to drink whenever he could, said it helped him forget." Her eyes flashed with tears. "It was like he'd given up on us."

He leaned across the table to grip her hand. Her fingers tightened in his. She smiled at him, wiped her face with her sleeve.

"I should be packing. Dad'll get into another rage if I don't clear the attic." She swallowed the last of her tea. "You'd better go."

"Couldn't I help you?"

"It's pretty mucky up there."

"I don't care." *Don't send me away.*

Dark shadows smudged beneath her eyes. "OK ... Thanks."

"Besides," he said. "You still haven't told me about your mum."

She gave a shaky laugh. "Ten out of ten for doggedness! In the attic ... I'll tell you all about it up there."

The room gaped grey and sad in the fading afternoon light. The easel stood empty on spindly skeleton legs. Shelves lay bare and dusty; boards stashed in sprawling heaps against the wall. Nathan ran his eyes round the attic, looking for a hidden exit, but nothing gave it away. Unless the triangular cupboard in the corner hid something ... But he could hardly open its doors to investigate.

"Could you clear those paints and put them in that box?" Rosalie kicked at an empty carton by the desk.

"Right." Nathan moved over to the shelf. "This is such a great room."

"Yes." She bent over some canvases. "Mum turned it from a junk room into a studio by putting in the two windows. When I was small I remember playing on the floor with crayons. Then after Dad went to prison and Mum became the real money earner, I began to paint seriously. I'd always been able to draw and it was like I could shut out the world, everything that was going wrong, if I had pencil and paper."

"And now you sell your stuff to Charlie?"

"Don't know what I'd do without him. He bought two of Mum's landscapes the week Dad went to prison. He put them in his shop window: *New Work by Moira Croft*. He sold them the same day. We never knew who bought them, but we were so grateful. We lived for months on the money."

"Will you be able to paint when you move?"

"Try to stop me! It's what I want to do when I leave school. Go to art college, like Charlie, get proper training." She straightened her back. "You see that chest on the back wall?"

Nathan looked across at a wide oak chest, its top littered with books.

"It's full of old artwork. When you've finished that shelf, could you pull everything out and heap it on the desk? I'll sort it tonight, see if anything is worth rescuing."

For twenty minutes they worked, Rosalie kneeling on the floor, sorting and sifting, Nathan lifting and carrying. They talked all the time. He told her about Dad and Karen and Amy, about Tom and their party – and about leaving all that for St Ives.

She was a good listener.

Then she told him how she'd been at school one morning in June, eighteen months ago, in the playground. "Suddenly the sky went dark and I heard Mum calling me."

Nathan stopped working and turned to look at her.

"I fainted. When I came to, her voice was still ringing in my head. I pushed everyone away from me and ran home, ran – I don't remember how I got here. I raced out to the bottom of the garden. Suddenly the calling stopped. I knew she was close."

"Go on."

"I climbed down to the plateau. One of the metal rungs had broken away and she must have slipped. She was lying there, all crumpled, blood on her face, her arms and legs like broken sticks." The girl's face puckered into a grim smile. "I told her she'd be OK, that I loved her. I raced here to ring for an ambulance. But by the time I got back to her, she was dead."

"I'm sorry –" The inadequate words stuck in his throat.

"Thanks." Tears stood in her eyes. "The strange thing is –"

"Tell me."

"I could never work out *why* Mum was on the cliff. If she'd gone out to the plateau to sketch something, as she did a lot, she'd have had her pencils and sketchbook with her. But she wasn't carrying anything – not even a bag. Just some housekeys in her pocket ... It was like she'd left the cottage in a hurry to go somewhere or meet someone ... Except we never ever found out where, or who it was."

"Afterwards," Nathan said gently, to fill the silence, "how did you cope?"

"The first few months were the worst. I didn't go back to school again that term and the summer was endless. When school started again I couldn't face it. The sympathy, the curiosity. It was like I was some kind of freak. One morning at school, I was in the loo and I heard the other girls talking about me. They'd given me a nickname: Spooky ... I started bunking off."

"Did your dad know?"

"I don't think he cared much where I was. He was grieving for Mum too, in his own way. He said his life was in a mess. So was mine, but I didn't have the heart to tell him."

"Didn't anyone help?"

"Yes." She stared out of the window. "Charlie spotted me one afternoon in November. I should have been at school, but instead I was hanging about on my own on the waterfront. He shut the shop and came out to me. We walked on the beach and ate a huge lunch in town. I was frozen and starving, the food was wonderful.

"Charlie told me he knew how hard everything was, but how I must stick it out at school, get through the exams, go to art college. It was like he could read my mind and healed something in it." She turned to look at him. "I went back to school the next day. I told my class teacher about the nickname, how much I hated it. I never heard it again. I worked like crazy to catch up, tried to make friends with everyone again. It was tough – but it was a lot easier than mucking about on my own." She bent over the canvases again. "That's the whole story, Sherlock."

She did not see the smile Nathan sent her across the room.

"Thanks for telling me," he said.

Ten minutes later, he'd reached the bottom drawer of the chest and knelt to pull it open. He looked at it more closely, checked it and looked again.

"Rosalie, this drawer."

"Yes?" She stood the other side of the attic, prodding the ceiling with a broom.

"It's got a false bottom. Come and see. If you look at it from the outside, the drawer's quite deep. But when you open it ... Look. This piece of wood's been laid halfway down."

She bent to inspect it. "Strange. Can we get it out?"

Nathan ran his hands round the inside of the drawer. "I'm not sure." His fingers scraped against a tiny clasp, then a second one. "Feel these. There ... and there."

She knelt beside him. He could feel the warmth of her. "Locks of some kind."

"Or they might be clasps that won't need a key." Nathan lay flat on the floor and peered dead level at the drawer. "I'll try to open them."

Rosalie stood up and backed away, her hands at her mouth.

He looked up at her. "What's the matter?"

"I'm frightened ... By what we might find."

"Don't you want to know what it is?"

"I've gone all shivery." She sat at the desk. "Go on, then."

Nathan ran his left hand along the piece of wood, felt the intricate metal of the clasp and flipped it open. His right hand struggled with the other clasp. "It's stuck." He persevered. The metal bit into his fingers. "OK, it's open."

He sat up. "Come and lift it away."

"Do it for me."

"Here. We'll do it together."

"Just do it, Nathan. Tell me what's inside."

He lay on the floor again, pulled at the wooden lining, pressed it and tried again. He managed to squeeze his fingers beneath it. He dragged it out.

"Well? Don't keep me in suspense." Her voice shook. "What's in there?"

Nathan craned his neck. "A sketchbook ... And a painting."
He felt a pang of disappointment.

Rosalie frowned. "Mum must have hidden them there.
Nobody else ever used that chest." She knelt beside him,
pulled out the sketchbook, turned its cover, stared down at
the first page.

She gasped.

She turned the second page, the third, the fourth.

Nathan looked over her shoulder at the delicate
charcoal drawings: heads, heads and shoulders; a naked
body sitting on the beach, running into the sea; hands,
hands and arms, sinewy legs and feet; heads again, turned
every which way, flowing in light and shade and shadow,
drawn with vivid tenderness.

"They're all of Charlie, aren't they?" Nathan said. "Every
single one."

Rosalie turned the pages until they got to the end.

"But he's younger in the first sketches ... look, there ...
These last ones, in coloured pencil, are later ... These have
all been drawn over many years, haven't they?"

"You're right." Thoughtfully, she sat back on her heels. "Over many years." She looked at Nathan. "I wonder ..."

"Yes?"

"Why were they hidden? And so carefully ... Mum obviously didn't want anyone to find them."

"Maybe she didn't want your dad to know Charlie was sitting for her?"

She held up the oil painting, gasped at its beauty. "This is Charlie too."

It was. The colours of the oils seemed to ripple towards them. Light from a wide background window fell on to Charlie's face, his penetrating blue eyes, his grey curls, the turn of his shoulders.

"It's one of the best portraits Mum ever did." Rosalie's hands shook. "I want Charlie to have it, for Christmas. As a special thank you."

"Are you sure?"

"Why?"

"If your mum hid it so carefully, maybe she never wanted anyone to see it – least of all Charlie."

"Well, *I* want him to."

He looked at her flushed face. "What about finishing the attic?"

"Tonight. I'll come back tonight." She zipped open a

wide leather case, packed the painting and the sketchbook into it. "Jesus, this is heavy."

"Let me carry it."

"Would you? Are you sure?"

"Of course." As he took the case from her, their hands brushed. The touch charged him with excitement.

"Let's go now. To the flat." Her eyes blazed at him. "Charlie's shop's bound to be open. He's going to get the biggest surprise of his life."

"You bet he is."

She flung her arms around him and her lips brushed his cheek. "Thank you for finding these."

He closed his eyes, desperate to kiss her mouth.

She pulled away. "Come on. Let's get down to the beach, before the dark."

They walked through the garden to the cliff edge. Nathan slung the bag over his shoulder, feeling its weight bite. Rosalie climbed swiftly down the ladder. She waited for him on the plateau, her hair blowing back from her face, her face pale against the darkening sky.

"I shall miss this," she said. "It's special for so many reasons."

Her voice faltered.

Nathan stood beside her. "Isn't this where you found your mum?"

"It took me weeks before I could bear to come out here again, or go down to the beach." She squared her shoulders. "Then Dad replaced the foothold where Mum had fallen, tested all the others to make sure they were safe ... I sit here and sketch in almost all weathers. You can see for miles, but nobody can see you."

"Like having your own private lighthouse." He gulped the air into his lungs, grateful for its sharpness. He looked over the cliff at the grey sea; then, sideways, at Rosalie's face and hair.

*I want to hold her hand, touch her hair, take her in my arms.*

She glanced at him as if she read his thoughts. "We'd better hurry. It'll soon be night."

They climbed the cliff face and started across the beach. Rock pools lay dark and murky. Long streaks of golden seaweed slid beneath their feet. Their shoulders brushed.

She slipped on some pebbles.

Instinctively he reached out to steady her. "Careful."

She smiled at him, twisted her fingers round his. He felt as if the two of them were linked now more deeply than the mere touching of hands. He heard only the dull roar of the sea, the gusting wind, the shrieks of wheeling gulls.

The silence of their voices slithered easily between them, as if suddenly they were friends.

At the end of the beach, they climbed up to the narrow street. The bustling crowds startled Nathan, the laughing chatter of voices, the shop lights, the bubbles of Christmas excitement he had totally forgotten.

Rosalie snaked through the crowds ahead of him. They turned down the street to the waterfront. Her voice cut through his thoughts. "Come on, we're here."

She stood by a shabby narrow door next to the fish and chip shop and kicked it open. They staggered up a cramped wooden staircase. Grim-faced, she opened the door.

The room was low-ceilinged, littered with boxes, piles of books and clothes. The smell of fish and stale beer hung in the air. A bay window looked bleakly over the waterfront, an archway led into a dingy kitchen. Another narrow flight of stairs trailed up to what Nathan supposed must be bedrooms.

"This is it." She flopped into a chair. "Hardly room to swing a cat. Tiggy isn't going to like it. I shall wait until the last moment before I bring her here."

Nathan slid the bag from his shoulder. Getting rid of its

weight was a relief, but his stomach clenched with the thought of leaving.

"Look," he said. "I'm starving. I bet you didn't have any lunch. Let's go and have tea in Kathy's Bar. Come on." He held out his hand.

She reached for it. "Great idea." She looked down at the bag. "Let me unpack the painting for Charlie. I can give it to him on the way."

She stooped over the bag and pulled out the painting. They stood for a moment admiring the thick oily colours glinting in the half-light.

And footsteps clumped on the stairs.

Rosalie gripped Nathan's arm. "That's Dad! I thought he'd gone to Penzance. Quick! Hide!"

"It's too late –"

Nathan turned to see Jake Croft's head and shoulders looming from the stairs. He lurched in the doorway, steadied himself against the wall.

"Well, *well*." The heavy lids drooped, almost closed with drink and tiredness. "If it isn't the lad from our back garden."

Nathan ran his tongue over his lips, backed away across the room.

"Afternoon, Mr Croft."

"Oh, you know who I am now, do you?" His head swayed. "So you *were* waiting for Ros that day!"

"Dad, this is Nathan. A friend of mine."

"*Is* he, indeed!" Her father gave a snort of laughter and turned to look at her. "What's that pretty picture you're holding?"

Rosalie clutched the painting more tightly.

"Come on, let's see it, then. Another trophy for the living-room?" He wrenched it from her and stared down at it. "What the hell is this?"

"You can see what it is." Her voice was cold, deliberate. "Mum's portrait of Charlie Ellis. Don't pretend you don't recognise him."

"Oh, I *recognise* him all right." Her father's face flushed and his eyes sparked livid with rage. "But I haven't seen *this* one before." He dropped it on the floor. "What's in that bag?"

"Nothing." Rosalie leaped towards it.

Her father shoved her out of his way. "No, you don't." He ripped at the bag, pulled out the sketchbook, flicked at the pages with stabbing fingers. "Charlie bloody Ellis, Charlie bloody Ellis." He said the words over and over, almost like a chant.

He looked at her, then across at Nathan, then down at

the drawings in his hands. He began to tear the paper into pieces, page by page, ripping and tearing like a demented vulture.

Rosalie gave a cry and tried to wrench the sketchbook away.

Her father turned on her. "Stop that! These are rubbish, do you hear? It's the past. It's all in the past. We've got to forget it ever happened, do you get me, girl?"

He picked up the oil painting. "And as for this," he raised his knee and smashed the painting against it. "*That*'s what I think of this!" He threw the canvas into the fireplace. "Tonight I'll light a fire. We can warm our hands on the blaze."

"No!" Rosalie raised her fists, threw herself against him. "That's Mum's work, her beautiful work. Don't you dare destroy it —"

"I dare all right, see if I don't." His huge hands grasped her arms as if they were matchsticks. "You've no right to bring that filth into this flat."

She flinched in pain, screamed, "It's not filth. How can you say that?"

"Everything's different now, do you hear? She's dead, your mother, and her work dies with her."

"Never! She'll never be dead. I can hear her, speak to her

... Let *go* of me –"

Her father released her. His voice dropped. "I said clear the attic, not trail its contents halfway across St Ives." He stared down at the torn sketches. "You're crazy, that's what you are. Talking to the dead."

"And you're nothing but a drunk." Nathan astonished himself as his own voice, rough with anger, burst across the room. "We've worked all afternoon to clear the attic for you. Rosalie's been in tears at leaving the place –"

Jake Croft turned towards him, his mouth slack with rage. "What's any of this got to do with you?"

"I offered to help Rosalie. We found those drawings of Charlie."

"Now look here." Jake Croft moved towards Nathan, raised his arm, brought it down on the side of Nathan's head. Nathan reeled over at the blow and crashed down against the wall. For a moment he could hear nothing but the boom of thunder in the sky.

"If you do that again," Rosalie's voice called across the room, clear and cold as a bell, "if you touch either of us again, I'll go to the police. I'm sick to death of your threats, your bullying. I'll tell the police exactly what you're like. Is that what you want?"

Nathan opened his eyes. From the floor, he saw Jake

Croft loom over Rosalie and raise an arm. He stood there swaying on his feet, like a scarecrow. Then he gave a sob of rage. His arm dropped.

He turned away, lurching, spitting on the torn sketches, trampling on them, kicking them aside.

His footsteps hurtled down the stairs.

Somewhere in the distance a door slammed.

"Don't cry." Nathan forced himself to stand. The floor swayed beneath him. He seemed to have bitten his tongue and his mouth tasted of blood. His head throbbed, drum-like, persistently.

He stumbled across the room and scooped Rosalie into his arms. "Everything will be all right," he said wildly. "I promise you. I'm going to the police. You can't go on like this –"

"No. Don't do anything." Her head was heavy on his shoulder, her voice low. "I'm going to run away."

"You can't do that." Nathan felt a stab of desperation. "It's a daft idea. It'll never work." He looked across at the grate, moved away from her, bent over the canvas and pulled it from the hearth. "The painting's torn, but we can still give it to Charlie."

She had slumped into a chair, her head in her hands.

"Don't give up, Rosalie. Think about your mum. What *she*'d want you to do."

She looked at the painting. "He's put his knee right through it. I can't possibly give that to Charlie."

"It's a clean tear," Nathan said lamely. "Maybe Charlie can mend it." He tried to flatten the canvas, join its centre together, knowing it was hopeless. He knelt beside her. "And we'll have tea in Kathy's Bar." He smoothed her hair away from her eyes. "If you let your dad get to you, he's won. Don't you see?"

She looked at him. "Did he hurt you?"

"No," he said, although his head throbbed. "Come on. Let's fight back."

"Good idea. Let's do that." She stood up unsteadily and began to scoop up the torn sketches. "Let's light the fire. Bring me the box of matches in the kitchen, by the stove. We're going to burn these sketches *and* the canvas."

"Are you sure?"

"Yes. Dad's wrecked all of them. But I won't give him the satisfaction of seeing Mum's work go up in flames."

They knelt beside the fire as piece by piece it nibbled at the edges of the sketches, consumed the hands, the faces, the writing bodies; scorched the canvas, curled its beauty into a blackened sooty mass smelling of burnt oil.

\* \* \*

They left the dying embers and walked out to the street, past the art shop.

Nathan stopped. "Your *Figures on a Beach*," he said. They stared at the empty space in the middle of the window. "It's gone."

She gripped his hand more tightly. "Maybe someone's bought it."

They peered in, saw Charlie wave and beckon.

"Rosalie ... and Nathan!" Charlie looked pleased. His eyes shone, his grey hair was ruffled. "I didn't know you'd met!"

"Only just," Nathan murmured, hot with sudden shyness. "At the cottage –"

"I'm delighted," Charlie said. "Have you seen her work? Paints like a dream, just like ... just like her mum." He looked at Rosalie. "I sold your *Figures on a Beach*. I was going to ring you. I put it in the window this morning and ... and someone bought it ... after lunch ... said it was just what they wanted." He clanged open the cash register, rustled some notes. "Here."

Rosalie gasped. "I can't believe it." She stared down at the bundle of money.

"It was good work, Rosalie. Excellent. You've come on no end since –" He bit his lip.

"Thank you so much, Charlie." She reached up to kiss his cheek. "You're a star."

For a split second Nathan thought he saw tears in Charlie's eyes.

"I'd do anything to help you." Charlie's voice was gruff. "Anything at all."

They stood outside the shop. Nathan hugged her. "Isn't that fantastic?"

Rosalie looked down at the notes in her hand. "Depends what you mean."

"How?"

She pushed the money into her pocket. "I can afford to run away now, can't I?"

"But I thought –"

"This feels like a sign, telling me I can go."

"*Please* don't –"

"It took me so long to get that painting right. Over and over again I tried. Now it's as if Mum's saying to me: It's the right time to leave."

"There's *never* a right time –"

"It's no good, Nathan. Dad's drinking's *much* worse. Ever since Mum died ... every day ... it's like there's a pattern ... month after month. It's been getting worse for eighteen months. I can't handle it any more." She looked at him, reached up to stroke the side of his head. "Him hitting *you* was the last straw."

He said bleakly, "I didn't mean to make things worse."

"You didn't. It's only a matter of time before he hits me too. I dread it ... Every morning I wake up and I'm scared ... Scared of being in the same room with him."

"Then let's go to the police. Tell them –"

She put a finger against his mouth. "I'm old enough to look after myself. I know I'm only fourteen, but if I tie my hair back, put on some make-up, I can look sixteen, no problem." She patted her pocket. "This money. It's more than I've ever earned. It'll keep me going for a bit."

"And when it runs out?"

"I'll find a job."

"You're too young! ... Can't we talk about it?"

"I'm sorry. I have to sort my things out, make supper for Dad so he doesn't suspect I'm leaving." She hesitated, her head tilted, her eyes closely inspecting him. "Of course, you could always come *with* me."

"Yes," Nathan said grimly. "I could. A couple of days ago I was so fed up I almost ran away myself." He pushed a hand through his hair. "But then I rang Dad ... He made me promise I wouldn't."

"I see." Her eyes flared with disappointment. "Well, a promise is a promise, isn't it?"

Briefly, unexpectedly, she hugged him, clung to his shoulder, her hair a mass of curls in his face. The scent of oil paint and honey seemed to fill his head.

"Goodbye, boy in the garden."

Before he could say anything she had turned away, walked down the waterfront towards the door of the flat. She waved and vanished inside.

He felt as if a massive fist had punched him in the stomach.

Nathan pushed against the crowds, struggled up the path through the dark woods to Tregenna. The air, colder, smelt of snow. The wind bit across his face.

*There was nothing I could do to change her mind. I called to her from the waterfront, saw her at the window, but she just shook her head. Wouldn't talk to me.*

"It's hardly surprising she wants to go, Weed. Having *him* for a dad ... How's your head?"

*Sore. I suppose it's a good thing he didn't give me a black eye. That would have taken some explaining.*

"Yeah. Be grateful for small mercies. So now what'll you do?"

*You tell me.*

"I'm going to have an early night," Mum said over supper. "I'm exhausted by that house-hunting. Tell Grandpa I'm sorry about the carols. I promise to come next year."

Nathan went back to his room and pulled on his boots and coat. He walked down the corridor to the lobby and pushed wearily at the main door.

A voice called, "Are you Nathan Fielding?"

He turned. "Yes?"

The girl at the desk gave him a professional smile. "I rang your room but there was no reply and I couldn't find you in the dining-room. Somebody left this for you twenty minutes ago."

A quiver of foreboding gnawed his stomach. "Do you know who it was?"

"She didn't leave her name. Pretty girl. Blonde."

"Thanks." He grabbed the small envelope and ripped it open. The handwriting streaked black and slanting.

*Dear Nathan*

*I'm sorry about Dad. I'm so ashamed of him. I don't want to give up on him but it seems to me I haven't got a choice. He doesn't want me. He'll probably be glad when I've gone.*

*You can't want to know any more about me. I'm packed and ready to go, the minute Dad leaves for the pub. He'll be so drunk when he gets back, he won't notice I'm gone until the morning, which gives me plenty of time to get away.*

*I hope you and your mum find a place to live. Thanks for your help today, boy in the garden. For finding Mum's sketches and the painting. I won't forget you.*

*Love  Rosalie*

Nathan stuffed the letter into his pocket. He pushed out of the hotel, gasping at the cold. The first flakes of snow danced into his eyes.

*She's dumped me, Banksie.*

"At least she took the trouble to write, to deliver the letter. Maybe she wants an answer."

*Nope. This is a straight goodbye. I really don't matter to her. I haven't make a blind bit of difference to her life. In fact, finding those sketches of Charlie might just have made everything worse.*

"How do you figure that out? Her dad was a drunk and a bully long before you came on the scene."

*Yes, but you didn't see his face when he looked at that painting. It was like someone had winded him, bruised him in the cruellest possible way.*

"Sure. His wife, Moira, and Charlie. They must have gone back a long way. There must have been something between them. Charlie must've spent more time naked with her than her husband did!"

*But now I'm never going to know, am I? We've lost the cottage and now I've lost Rosalie ... Do you know what, Banksie?*

"What?"

*I've never felt so useless in my life.*

The church smelt of snow-dampened coats, sherry and candle wax. Grandpa wove his way through the crowd to sit with the choir. Nathan sat numbly at the end of a pew, listening to the organ, the low murmur of voices. Small candles, built into white paper plates, passed from hand to hand, flickering into life as they were lit. Reflections of the flames danced in people's eyes and huge shadows leaped across the walls.

Nathan remembered the candlelit attic.

*If only I were in it now with Rosalie.*

The service began. Rustling, clearing their throats, the congregation stood for 'Once in Royal David's City'. Nathan sang, hearing his own voice interweaving. The choir trilled 'Mary Had a Baby'. A chorister read the first lesson.

Nathan stopped listening. He stood automatically to sing.

*The holly and the ivy, when they are both full grown*

He thought about Dad in Edinburgh, about Tom, about tonight's party in London.

*For of all the trees that are in the wood, the holly bears the crown*

Everything there seemed so remote, like a separate world.

*The rising of the sun and the running of the deer*

He thought about Rosalie. His fingers tightened on the letter in his pocket.

*The playing of the merry organ, sweet singing in the choir*

And he knew what he had to do.

The carol ended. Rustling, everyone sat. Nathan remained standing. He caught sight of Grandpa's tanned face, his white tuft of hair. Then he clenched his fists, stepped hurriedly into the aisle and began to walk towards the back of the church. Eyes fastened on him, curious, full of song.

An arm reached out. "Nathan." Charlie's deep burr. "Is anything wrong?"

Nathan stopped. "No. I'm fine, Charlie, thanks. But could you tell Grandpa." His voice cut into the hush. "I'm going back to Tregenna. He's not to worry."

He ran towards the church door, reached for the iron handle, twisted it and pulled. Reluctantly, the door opened. Gusts of frosty air swirled into his face. He looked back. The candles dipped, flickered wildly, almost blew out. Vast shadows somersaulted across the walls. Faces turned to look at him, impatient, startled from their rituals.

He slipped through the door, hauled it shut and heard it clang into the night.

\* \* \*

The snow fell silently and methodically, lying in contented drifts on the streets. Nathan pulled up his hood. His boots crunched. The flakes spattered then melted on his shoulders.

He'd had an idea which just might stop Rosalie leaving.

He slithered down the hill past Kathy's Bar and rounded the corner to the waterfront. He found the fish and chip shop and the door to the flat. He stood back from it, looking up at the bay window, then at the square of pale light from the second storey window. A bedraggled curtain looped across it. He longed for her to open it, to look out. The snow fell relentlessly into his eyes.

He heard footsteps clumping down the stairs. He ducked quickly into a doorway. Jake Croft shot out on to the street. "I'm going to the pub," he shouted. "Don't you go back to the cottage. Do you hear me, girl? You stay right here where I can find you."

He slammed the door.

Nathan shrank further into the shadows. Jake Croft walked heavily past him, lighting a cigarette. He moved down the waterfront and turned sharp right.

Nathan looked up at the bay window.

*I must see her.*

He crashed against the door.

Footsteps flapped on the stairs, the door creaked open.

"Nathan? What are you *doing* here?"

*She's got her coat on. She's all ready to leave.*

She pulled him into the narrow hall. "Are you mad? He'll kill you if he finds you here again. He's still livid. Didn't say a word to me all evening ... He's just left –"

"I know. I saw him. *Listen* to me for a moment. Please don't run away."

"Didn't you get my letter? I trailed all the way up to Tregenna with it."

"Yes, I've got it here."

"That said it all."

He looked into her eyes. "Did it?"

She hesitated. Then she said, "I told you. I've made up my mind."

He took a deep breath. "Look. I've had an idea. Your dad doesn't care *who* he sells the cottage to. Right?"

"I suppose. As long as he gets the money –"

"Exactly!" Nathan clenched his fists. "So what if he sells it to us. To Mum and me. And you come to live with us?"

*"What?"*

"It'd solve everything. Mum and me would get the cottage. You could stay in your own home. Your dad would get his money. Brilliant or what?"

Rosalie shook her head. "Your mum'd never agree. Why would she want me to live with you?"

"Because *I* do." Nathan choked over the words. "That attic. It's *your* room. Your space. I want you to go on living there." He flushed. "And there's something else."

"What?"

"I didn't want to move down here. When Mum first told me, I was so angry I wanted to hit her."

"Because of leaving London?"

"Yes, and not being with Dad and Tom." He swallowed. "But I wouldn't mind it so much if we can live in your cottage. Mum knows that. I reckon if I ask her about you, she'll agree. She wants to make things better for me."

Rosalie looked at him. "You're in cloud-cuckoo-land. You can't blackmail your mum like that. Dad would never give me to someone else's family. He's got his pride, even if he is a drunk ... Anyway, you know the cottage is sold."

"Couldn't we stop the sale?" He ran a hand through his hair. "Surely there's still time? If we talk to your dad and then to Mum, we –"

Rosalie shook her head. "No. Nice try, Nathan, but I must go. My bag's packed. If I don't leave now ..."

"Will you think about what I've said? Please?"

"Yeah. On the motorway."

"Why won't you tell me where you're going?"

"Because you'll come looking for me, that's why!"

He looked at her standing there, clenched, shivering. He noticed a leaflet sticking out of her coat pocket, a bus timetable or something. "So where *are* you going?"

"I'm not telling you, so don't ask. You're wasting your breath."

"Rosalie." Nathan gripped her arm. "What about school and your exams – and art college. How will you do all that if you –?"

"Couldn't care *less* about it –"

Nathan knew that wasn't true. He persevered. "Your dad will be furious if you leave. He'll get the police on to you. If they find you and bring you back, things here will be worse for you. Much worse."

"He won't bother to track me down. He'll never find me."

"Then you'll spend the rest of your life on the run. On the streets, sleeping rough. Is that what you want?"

Rosalie slid away from him. "I know you're trying to help. But I can look after myself. Please. Leave me alone."

"Then will you ring me?" He grabbed her hand, scrabbled in his pocket for a biro. "Look, here's my number." He scrawled it on to her wrist. "There ... Promise you'll ring. We'll be home on Boxing Day. If there's anything I can do –"

She hesitated. "There is something –"

"What?"

She bent her head and raised her arms. She unclasped the silver necklace with the oval jade-green stones.

"Look after this for me." She put it into his hands. The stones, warm from her skin, glowed in the half-light.

"Mum gave it to me the Christmas before she died. It's the most precious thing I have. Keep it safe for me, boy in the garden."

She pushed him towards the door.

"Now go."

Nathan looked out over the waterfront. Snowflakes danced into the murky water, frazzled the surface and vanished. His legs ached, his head throbbed. Hot tears of disappointment dribbled down his face.

*I'll never see her again. She'll never ring me, I know she won't. All I've got is a letter and a necklace.*

His fingers tightened on the precious stones in his pocket. He stabbed at the tears with his sleeve, hunched into his coat and pulled the hood over his head.

*It's over. I give up.*

He glanced round at her bay window. The light flicked out. He cursed under his breath, then turned and started to march away, across the waterfront, up the street Jake Croft had taken.

He dipped his face against the snow, dragged himself up the narrow hill. He heard the babble of voices, laughter, jazz, someone singing at a piano: the sounds floated towards him on the soft, icy flakes. They made him feel sick.

He looked up to the end of the street. A pub stood on the corner. The lamps at its windows glittered gold and orange on the snow. A group of men flung themselves out of the door, one after another, elbows pushing, legs kicking, their faces gold and orange under the light.

"Your word!" A voice from the group came coarse and furious. "Don't give me that bullshit, Croft. How can we take your word for anything?"

"Thinks we were born yesterday."

"Came down in the last shower."

"Trying to talk his way out of it again."

"Yeah. We've heard it all before, haven't we?"

"Every excuse under the sun."

More pushing.

"A promise is a promise."

A green hat bobbed pathetically in the centre of the circle. "I tell you," Jake Croft shouted to be heard, his voice slurring. "You'll get it all back and with interest. I just need a bit more time. After Christmas, fellas, I give you my –"

"We're sick to death of waiting."

"Don't say we didn't warn you –"

For a split second the group froze. Then all the arms seemed to be raised. Legs kicked. Voices howled. The chink of metal rang into the street, a fierce glint of light flashed from a single hand.

The green hat disappeared.

The group huddled together, looked down at the pavement, at the body sprawled at their feet.

"That was a knife."

"Who had a knife?"

"What the hell've you done?"

"Is he dead?"

Silence again, a whole frozen moment of terror.

Then the group broke up, pushing, shoving, leaping right and left. Legs ran, every which way.

The street emptied.

The lamps from the pub shone over the body.

12

Nathan stood paralysed in the snow. He seemed to be the only person on the hill, in the whole of St Ives, in the entire universe.

A piano tinkled from a nearby window and a child's voice started to sing:

*Oh little town of Bethlehem*
*How still we see thee lie ...*

A sob broke from Nathan's throat. He dragged himself towards the body. The green hat lay crumpled beside it. Nathan knelt down and closed his eyes. He smelt blood on the snow, sweat on the man's skin. He forced himself to look.

Jake Croft lay slumped on his side. A bright red river trailed from his neck, melting the snow, dribbling away. His mouth gaped open as if in surprise. His eyes, half closed, squinted up at Nathan.

"Lad. Help me, lad." The mouth seemed to struggle with an enormous tongue. "Did you see what happened? Don't leave me. You must help me, lad. Please."

*But I want to run. That's all I want. To run away from this as fast as I can. Except my legs won't move and I can't. I can't leave him. This is Rosalie's dad. He might be dying. How can I leave him like this?*

He wrenched off his coat and draped it over the man's body. Then he remembered. Carefully, he pulled Rosalie's letter and necklace from the coat, tucked them separately into the pockets of his jeans.

He bent towards Jake's face. "It's all right. You're going to be all right."

He took one of Jake's hands. It was burning hot, wet with sweat, huge and heavy, urgent in its clasp. "I'll get help. You're going to be OK."

Snow soaked through his sweater on to his back. Blood seeped from the pavement into his jeans. He heard voices beside him, a young couple. He looked up at them.

"Are you all right? Is he badly hurt? What happened?"

"I don't know," Nathan's voice shook. "I found him lying here."

"Is he dead?"

"No. But I don't know how bad he is. He must've been in a fight. He needs help. Quickly. Could you ring for an ambulance? Please? From the pub?"

"Sure. Hold on there. We'll be right with you."

The couple vanished inside.

Nathan bent over Jake Croft. "They've gone to get help. An ambulance will take you to hospital. You'll be OK." The grip on his hand slackened. "Can you hear me? I'm leaving to find Rosalie, before she ... to tell her what's happened."

He picked up the green hat.

Jake's heavy lids, like thick cheese, drooped over his eyes.


*How do I find Rosalie before it's too late? Should I go back to the flat?*

"No. She said her bag was packed, she was ready to go."

*So what do I do? Where should I go?*

"Think it out, Weed. You need to get to the bus station. Start looking for her there."

*What if the bus has already left? What if Jake dies?*

"What if, what if. Just get a move on. Take it step by step."

*The bus station. I don't even know where it is.*

"Yes, you do. Don't panic. Get on to the road to Tregenna. It's on the left-hand side, where the road bends. You've passed it a hundred times."

*Right.*

"Keep going, Weed. Carefully does it. Don't slip in the snow."

*He saw me, Banksie. Jake Croft saw me. He spoke to me. I held his hand. There's blood all over my jeans. His blood.*

"*I know.*"

Nathan lumbered round the corner, past Collins Estate Agents, a greengrocer, a newsagent, an antiques dealer: the row of shops was never-ending. His legs felt heavy, as if he were trapped in a dream, unable to move. Panting, he reached the top of the road to Tregenna. He saw the small coach park on his left.

It seemed to be empty.

Perhaps all the buses had left for the night.

He looked again. A single bus turned on its lights and revved its engine. It hiccuped and died. The driver tried again, raised an arm, adjusted the mirror, checked the controls.

Nathan raced towards it. The bus began to move. It passed him, swung slowly out on to the road. A group of passengers clustered near the front. The rest of the bus was empty. His heart sank. Then he saw a girl with fair curly hair sitting at the back.

"No!" Nathan screamed. "Stop! Please! Stop!"

He staggered into the road in front of the bus, waving his arms, waving a blood-spattered hat.

Rosalie glanced out at him. She pressed her face to the window. She saw Nathan. She saw what he was waving. Surprise and then alarm cracked across her face. She stood up, yelling to the driver. He seemed not to hear. The bus moved on. The girl lurched down the aisle to the front.

The bus ground to a halt, snow slushing around its wheels.

The driver opened his window. "Idiot!" he yelled.

"I'm sorry." Nathan's breath seemed trapped in his lungs. "I must talk to –"

Rosalie stood at the door of the bus.

It opened.

"That's Dad's hat."

"Thank God I caught you in time."

"It's covered in blood. Where's your coat? What's happened?"

"There's been an accident. Outside the pub. They're ringing for an ambulance."

She turned to the driver. "Will you let me off?"

"Move, then. You're holding everybody up." He leaned across the wheel and glared out at Nathan. "Don't you *ever* try that stunt again."

Rosalie grabbed her bag and slid down the steps.

The bus rumbled away up the hill.

She looked at him. "There's blood on your jeans."

"Yes."

"Is it Dad's?"

He took her arm, steadied her against him, told her all he knew.

"He's been asking for it." The bitterness in her voice alarmed him. "He owes money everywhere. He plays on people's goodwill until –" She looked at him. "What am I going to do?"

"Let me take you back to the flat. Leave your bag there. We'll ring for a taxi."

"To go where?"

"To take you to the hospital."

"You mean, I have to see him?"

"Yes, Rosalie, you do."

She suddenly looked much younger. "So there's no running away for me tonight?"

"Not now, not ever."

He heard his own words and thought, *Running away never solves anything, does it? Sooner or later you just have to face the same stuff all over again. The trouble is, Mum's running away from London, but I've got to go with her.*

He pushed Rosalie's hair out of her eyes and touched her cheek. It felt cool beneath the heat of his fingers.

"Come on. Let's get you home." He swung an arm around her shoulder.

Then he remembered.

Gently, he pulled the necklace from his pocket, held the clustered stones in his palm. "Put this back on."

She faced him. Flakes of snow fell on her face, sparkled on her lashes. "Do it for me. I'm shaking like a leaf."

He fumbled with the clasp, his hands beneath her hair, on the warmth of her neck.

He stood back and smiled. "It looks much better on you," he said, "than it did on me."

He woke the next morning feeling lumpy and sore. An egg-like swelling bulged beneath his hair on the side of his head.

*What a delightful present, Mr Croft. Thank you very much. If Mum notices it, you'll have something to answer for.*

He'd left his jeans to soak in the bath the night before. He rinsed them out. The smell of dirt, stale beer and old blood turned his stomach. He pulled on his swimming trunks and bath robe, then limped along the corridor to the pool.

*Tonight's Christmas Eve. I've never felt less like Christmas in my life. It's as if it hardly matters any more. I wonder how the party went last night. I must ring Tom and find out.*

He pushed at the door to the pool. It stretched long and flat, its turquoise water barely moving. He walked across the cool tiles, raised his arms and dived.

*It's weird being the only swimmer. I expect everyone is still in bed.*

*I wonder how Rosalie is. And Jake. I'll have to ring the hospital, tell them I'm a relative, try to get some news.*

He thrashed up and down the length of the pool. As he pulled himself out of the water, he saw a girl standing the other side of the glass partition, her eyes heavy with exhaustion.

*Rosalie.*

He raced for his towel, his feet slipping on the tiles. He ran out to meet her, uncomfortably aware of his skinny, angular body, the wet hair clinging to his forehead, the goose pimples shivering his arms.

"Hi." Her face was pale, her voice low. "I had to see you."

"How is he?"

"They operated last night. He'd lost a lot of blood but he's been lucky. He's going to be OK."

"Thank God for that ... You look terrible."

"Thanks! They gave me a bed next to his but I couldn't sleep." Tears filled her eyes. "You should have seen him, Nathan. He looked so sad and old."

"I *did* see him," he reminded her. "I know what he looked like. I'll never forget."

"Yes, of course." She bit her lip. "I do love him, you know, in spite of everything."

Nathan shrugged. "He's your dad. Of course you love him, whatever he's done."

He stared at Rosalie's tired face. He saw her lips moving, but for a moment he couldn't hear what she said, only the sound of his own words echoing in his head, giving themselves new meaning.

*And I love my dad. Whatever he's done. Whatever he's doing right now and whoever he's with. He'll always be my dad, even if other people get in the way. Other things ...*

"Nathan? Are you OK?"

He jumped. "Sorry?"

"Dad wants to see you. That's what I came to say."

*"What?"*

"He remembers everything. He's so grateful to you for not just leaving him lying there, after the way he treated you. He wants to say sorry." She looked almost too tired to talk. "And he's got something to tell you."

"I'm not sure I want –"

"Please? It'll be worth your while." She hesitated. "You remember that prayer we said together in the attic?"

It seemed like years ago. "Yes?"

"I can't tell you any more now. Just please come."

He took pity on her. "OK. For you. When I think about how he's treated you –"

"He says he'll stop drinking. He says I'm to throw out all the booze in the flat, so he can make a fresh start. He says –"

Impatience with the man welled up in Nathan. "Do you believe him?"

She met his eyes. "If I don't, who will?"

"I suppose." Hunger clawed at his stomach. "Have you had breakfast?"

"No."

"How does bacon and eggs sound?"

"Fantastic."

"Give me five minutes to get dressed."

She glanced at his bare chest. Something in the shyness of her smile made Nathan blush.

It was not until the fragrance of cooked breakfast curled beneath his nose that Nathan realised just how hungry he was. It felt extraordinary, having Rosalie beside him, introducing her to Mum, watching them instantly take to each other.

They told Mum briefly how they'd met at the cottage,

how he'd been helping Rosalie clear the attic, about Jake's accident.

"I was walking back after the carols," Nathan said, deftly spinning a story to leave out the bit about Rosalie's plan to run away. "I just happened to find him outside the pub. I got some people to ring for an ambulance, told Rosalie about him. And now he wants to thank me. Would it be OK if Rosalie and I go to the hospital? I promise I won't be long."

"That'll be fine," Mum said. "I'll meet you back here at midday. I'm house-hunting again. It's my last chance to find something." She looked at Rosalie. "Will you be on your own tomorrow?"

Rosalie flushed. "I suppose I will, now that Dad's –"

"We can't have that. Not on Christmas Day. Come and have lunch with us. At my dad's house in Bowling Green Terrace. Number twenty-two."

Rosalie's face lit up. "Are you sure?"

"Positive. He'll be delighted to meet you – delighted that Nathan's made a friend." She poured herself another cup of tea. "Let's say one o'clock. That'll give you time to see your dad in hospital and then come on to us."

"Thank you very much, Mrs Fielding. I'll check with Dad. But I'd love to."

"Thanks, Mum." Nathan looked across at her. "That's really nice of you."

She gave him a sudden, dazzling smile.


Nathan and Rosalie stood together at the end of Jake Croft's bed. He lay sleeping, his head and neck heavily bandaged, his mouth purple, his skin pallid.

Rosalie moved towards him and touched his hand. "Dad?"

He stirred, muttered, opened his eyes. "Ros." He tried to sit up. "Where –?"

"Don't try to move, Dad. I've brought Nathan to see you."

"Yeah, sure." The head rolled back on to the pillow. "Good girl." The dark eyes glinted up at Nathan from their heavy lids. "Wanted to say thanks."

Nathan swallowed back a mixture of anger and pity. "I was in the right place at the right time. That's all."

"No. It was good of you to stay with me. Not many would've bothered." Jake's hand clawed at the sheet. "Your coat. They're cleaning it up for you."

"Right. I'll ask one of the nurses ..."

There was an awkward pause.

"Good of you to come," Jake said. "I need to ask you something. Something important ... " His voice trailed away.

"Yes?"

"Those men who ..."

"Yes."

Jake seemed to make an enormous effort to speak. "You never saw them. Not them, nor the knife. If the police ask you, tell them you came across me lying there. But you never saw the fight. Get it?"

"You mean –?"

"Yeah. I know why they beat me up. Know only too well. But I'll not give the police their names. I'll not press charges."

"But one of them –"

"I know. Could've been murder. I'm bloody lucky. Thing is –" more clawing, "if I tell the police, it'll never end. I'll never be able to live in St Ives again. But if I leave it, pay back the money I owe them once I've sold the cottage, they'll feel they've had their revenge." His voice faltered. "And maybe Ros and I can get on with our lives in peace."

*So Rosalie might have been in danger too?*

*I can't bear the thought of that. I'll have to do what he asks.*

"It's your decision, Mr Croft. I'll go along with whatever you want."

"Good lad ... Thanks." Jake sighed with relief, his hand relaxed. "Could I have some water?"

Rosalie held the glass to her dad's mouth. He slurped at the liquid.

"Wish there was a drop of whisky in that!" He grinned faintly at her.

"Well, there isn't," Rosalie said firmly. "And there won't be!"

"I know, I know. Only the tasteless stuff from now on."

Rosalie put down the glass. "Dad, there's something else you wanted to tell Nathan. Remember? About the cottage –"

"Oh, sure." Jake's eyes glinted at him again. "Ros tells me you and your mum want to buy it."

Surprise tingled down Nathan's spine. "Your house?"

"That's right."

"I ... we –" he spluttered. "Well, yes, of course –"

"A Mrs Fielding rang me a couple of days ago. Is she your mum?"

"That's right. She ... we –"

"She offered me the asking price. Is that right or was I just dreaming?"

"No. I mean yes. That's right. We wanted to buy it very much." Nathan swallowed. "You said it was sold."

"Thought it was. Thought I had the money in the bag." Jake shifted his body beneath the sheets. The smell of disinfectant rose from the starch.

"Mum's been looking for something else all over St Ives." Nathan felt colour flood his cheeks. "She's not found anything she likes."

Jake's hand brushed the air, as if to shut Nathan up. "Then the bloody woman who was buying it – what do you think she did, eh? What *do* you think she did?"

Nathan's tongue seemed to stick to the roof of his mouth. "I've no idea."

"She let me down, the silly cow, that's what she did."

*"What?"*

"Yeah. Rang me at the flat yesterday morning. I was just off to Penzance to talk to a mate of mine about some work. She said she'd found somewhere else with a smaller garden. Said she was worried about the cliff, what with the baby and all. Said she couldn't be too careful." He gave a wheezy cough. "'Course, I reckon some loud-mouth told her about my wife's accident ... Warned her off."

"Was that why –?"

"Yeah. I crashed out of the flat, got myself well and truly plastered." He licked his lips. "Shouldn't have taken it out on you and Ros ... What I'm trying to say, lad, is that if you still want it –"

*"Still want it!"*

"You and your mum can buy our cottage." Mr Croft

searched for Rosalie's hand again, as if it were his lifeline. "We don't want to have to sell up, but I must pay off those debts of mine –"

"Mr Croft! Mum will be over the moon."

*Our prayer ... It worked!*

He met Rosalie's eyes and knew she was thinking exactly the same.

*The attic. I'll have the attic. Rosalie can come there. We'll climb down to the plateau together, sketch there, swim from the beach.*

*Tom can stay. At half-term. I'll ask him for half-term.*

"OK." Jake gave him the faintest grin. "Consider it a done deal. Soon as I'm out of this place, I'll get things moving."

Rosalie leaned towards her father. "Dad?"

"Yes, Ros."

"I met Nathan's mum this morning. At Tregenna. She gave me breakfast."

"That was good of her."

"I told her about your accident –"

"Not the truth, I hope?"

"No. Only that you'd been hurt."

"That's my girl."

"She's asked me to Christmas lunch tomorrow at Nathan's grandfather's."

"That's nice of her, too, what with me stuck in here."

"Can I go, Dad? You won't mind if I go?"

"'Course not." His eyes closed. "Go and enjoy yourself ... Give me another swig of that tasteless stuff, there's a good girl."

Nathan waited at Tregenna for Mum. He'd left Rosalie with her dad; rescued his coat from one of the nurses. Now he paced the front of the hotel, watching the last vans deliver Christmas food, flowers, wine, the new arrivals drive up, travel weary, just in time for Christmas Eve. The sea heaved and glittered under the midday sun. Drifts of snow released their whiteness into melting patches of sharp green lawn.

He spotted Mum walking across the path and raced towards her.

"Good news at last," she said. "I've found us somewhere to live."

"No, you haven't."

"There's a pretty house out along the road to Carbis Bay."

"No, there isn't."

"It's expensive but I think we can afford it."

"No, we can't."

"I want you to come and see it this afternoon."

"No, you don't."

She frowned. "Why not, Nathan?"

"Because, because, the Wizard of Oz."

"Why are you behaving like a drunken bumblebee?"

"I'll give you three guesses."

"Nathan –" she began warningly.

"Come on, Mum. Guess." He flapped his arms, circled around her, zoomed away and back again. "In your wildest dream. Something's happened."

"What?"

"Something terrific." Zoom.

"I've no idea what you're on about."

"Then I'll have to tell you." Double zoom.

"Nathan, slow down. You're making me dizzy."

"Remember that cottage I found? Rosalie's cottage?"

"How can I forget?"

"It's ours if we want it."

Mum stopped plodding. *"What?"*

"Jake Croft's just told me. From his hospital bed."

"But he'd sold it to –"

"The buyer changed her mind."

"You mean –?"

"She pulled out. Yesterday."

Mum gazed at him, rooted to the spot. "I don't believe it."

"True as I'm standing here. Wonderful or what?"

Colour flooded Mum's face. Then she yelled with delight. She scooped off her beret, threw it in the air, flung herself at Nathan and caught him in her arms.

They began to bob along the sandy path, two small figures twirling beneath the sun.

Nathan rang Tom that evening, on Christmas Eve. The party had gone well, Tom said, but it hadn't been the same without him. Nathan quickly told him the news about the cottage and asked him to come down to St Ives for half-term.

"We can do tons of things here," Nathan said. "It won't be warm enough to swim but we can go on the beach and stuff, and you can meet Rosalie and –"

Tom hadn't needed any persuading. He went to check with his mum and came back to the phone a minute later. "You're on, Weed! Mum says she can't wait to see the back of me!"

Nathan was just about to leave his room minutes later when the phone rang.

"I wanted to surprise you," Dad said. "There are presents for you in that basket from Karen and Amy and me, but I wanted to give you something extra special this year. For being such a great kid and coping with everything."

Nathan tried to say it was OK but the words stuck in his throat.

"I've been meaning to say this for ages and I'm going to say it now. In September. When I left. I should've told you about Karen before I went. It was horrible and cowardly of me and I'm sorry. Leaving Mum to tell you on my behalf was a rotten thing to do. Just because she's so brilliant at dealing with other people's problems, I shouldn't have taken it for granted that she could handle her own the same way."

Nathan coughed and swallowed.

"Nat?" Dad asked sharply. "Have you got a cold?"

"No," Nathan snuffled. "I'm fine –"

"Thank God for that!" Dad said. "Because you and me, we're going somewhere special for the New Year. Just the two of us. I'm taking you to Switzerland, to St Moritz. You're going to learn to ski!"

"Dad! That's fantastic!" This time the words didn't get a chance to stick. "I can't wait!"

"Neither can I ... You've been great, Nat. I'm really proud of you. Mum told me about the cottage and everything and I'm just so pleased it's what you want. When the time comes, I'll come down to help you move in."

"You will?"

"Of course. Mum says the cottage is beautiful and I'm

dying to see it."

"Us being so far away. Will it matter?"

"Not a jot. I refuse to let it get in the way of us seeing each other, I promise ... Nat?"

"I'm still here –"

"Have you opened the presents yet?"

"No. They're in Mum's room. We're taking them to Grandpa's tomorrow."

"Well, when you see what mine is, you'll understand its special purpose ... Happy Christmas, Nat. Love you loads."

While Grandpa and Mum put the finishing touches to Christmas lunch, Nathan sat on the floor by Grandpa's Christmas tree in a sea of wrapping paper, Charlie in the armchair by the fire.

Dad had given him a winter coat, light as a feather and ideal for skiing; Karen a mobile phone with the message *Ring us any time.*

*She feels guilty that she's stolen my dad,* thought Nathan.

He remembered what he'd said to Mum, that morning she'd broken the news: that Dad would always be somewhere else, on the end of a stupid phone. And now here he was, sitting with it in his lap. But he supposed Karen was only trying to be friendly. She could be a whole lot worse ... And he'd be able to ring a lot of other people with it, as well as Dad.

Amy had made him some splodgy biscuits, sticky with chocolate chips. Nathan bit into one. It wasn't bad – for a smarmy brat, anyway...

Mum had given him a huge polo-neck sweater which Nathan pulled on. He was so hot in it he could hardly breathe. Charlie said he looked like an Arctic explorer and asked which mountain he intended to conquer. He'd given Nathan a set of oil paints. "I expect to see excellent work with those!" Nathan put them happily with Grandpa's art-shop haul.

When the doorbell rang, Nathan leaped from the floor and rushed to answer it. Rosalie held out a bunch of irises. "I hope these will be all right. I bought them at the hospital. I haven't had time to do any shopping –"

"Nor me." Nathan pulled her into the hall. "It's you we want to see, not the contents of the shops." He took the flowers and her jacket. She wore a turquoise sweater, the jade necklace. The scent of oil paint and honey clung to her. "You look great."

"I slept for ten hours last night."

"How's your dad?"

"On the mend." She paused at the door to the living-room.

"Charlie! What a lovely surprise."

Charlie, already on his feet, looked stunned. "Rosalie!"

Nathan told him briefly about Jake's accident and why Rosalie was with them. Charlie's eyes darkened with rage.

"You should've let me know." He moved towards her. "I'd no idea anything had happened. It's been Christmas pandemonium in the shop. I didn't shut it until nine o'clock last night."

"Thanks, Charlie, but there was nothing you could've done. Dad's been asking for trouble. Of course, I didn't *want* the fight to happen, but in a way I'm glad it's all come to a head."

"We're buying Rosalie's cottage," Nathan burst out, frightened by the anger in Charlie's face, wanting to smooth it away. It seemed to work, though when they sat down to talk, Charlie's eyes were constantly on Rosalie, worried, thoughtful, as if there were many other things he wanted to say.

Nathan looked around the faces at the Christmas table.

Grandpa, flushed with cooking the most delicious turkey in the world — "Does anyone want any more?" — a paper hat perched on his tufty hair — "There's still a trifle, you know, and I couldn't bear it for breakfast."

Mum, relaxed, happy, wearing the orange scarf Nathan had given her –"Dad, we'll not need to eat for a week" – speaking to Max on the phone, handing the phone to Nathan –"He wants to say hello again" – throwing back her head with laughter at one of the jokes in a cracker –"The old ones are still the best!"

Charlie, his lean face eager now, the thoughtfulness banished, as if he had come to a decision, his hands restless, gesturing –"And this is what you look like, Henry, in that hat" – drawing a cartoon of Grandpa on his serviette with a few deft flicks of his pen.

Rosalie –"Wish I could sketch like that" – looking at Charlie and then at the drawing, smiling at Nathan whenever their eyes met across the table.

Grandpa filled their glasses. "I want to drink a toast. To all my guests. God bless you for being with me." He hiccuped loudly. "To health, happiness and Christmas."

His hat slipped to the floor.

There was a ripple of laughter and murmured approval. Everybody drank.

Charlie raised his glass again. The crimson liquid glinted. His eyes met Rosalie's. And it seemed to Nathan that a hush fell across the room like the shadow of a giant hand. Nobody spoke or moved. The lanterns on the tree flickered. A log cracked in the grate.

"May you never thirst," Charlie said.

Rosalie stood up. Her glass tipped sideways. Wine trickled its thin bright frond across the tablecloth. "What did you say?"

Charlie's eyes never left hers. "May you never thirst."

"Mum used to say that."

"I know."

"It was her special blessing. For people she loved."

"Yes, Rosalie, I know."

"I've never heard anyone else use it."

"She often said it to me."

Rosalie stepped back from the table. "What do you mean, Charlie? What are you trying to say?"

Charlie stood up. "Can't you guess?"

Rosalie's hands went to her mouth as if to catch her words. None came. She turned away from him and ran into the hall.

Charlie flung back his chair, muttered an apology and followed her.

Nathan glanced at Mum and Grandpa's startled faces. There was an uncomfortable silence.

Nathan filled it by saying quickly, "It's OK. I guess they've got stuff to sort out ... Great lunch, Gramp."

"Fantastic," Mum said. "I can't believe what a marvellous cook you've become. You'll have to try all those fish recipes in the book Nathan's just given you."

But Grandpa wasn't listening. "Wait a minute." He frowned. "I wonder ... I've just put two and two together. Well, I'll be ... Charlie Ellis is a dark horse and *no* mistake. *There's* a turn-up for the books –"

Nathan had no idea what Grandpa was on about. He could hear the quiet voices in the hall. Charlie, talking and talking, Rosalie interrupting, her voice high, asking questions. But he couldn't make out the words.

Curiosity overwhelmed him. He stood up. "Just going to find out what's going on."

He slipped quickly to the doorway.

"My dream," he heard Rosalie say. "The dream that's haunted me and that I tried to paint. Those figures on a beach. Mum walking with a man, but I never knew who he was. She's with *you*, Charlie, isn't she? Somewhere in the back of my mind, I must've remembered seeing you together."

"Yes." Charlie's voice was low. "When you brought the painting into the shop, I couldn't believe my eyes. It wasn't just that it's the best thing you've ever done. It seemed to me it was also a sign you were ready ..."

He moved towards her.

She threw back her head. "No. No closer. Don't come any closer, do you hear?"

She ran for the door.

Nathan stepped into the hall. "Rosalie —"

"I'm sorry, Nathan. I can't stay a minute longer." She reached for her jacket, flung it over her shoulders.

The front door swallowed her.

Nathan said, "What's happened, Charlie? Why has she run off?"

"It's for her to tell you, not me." Charlie's voice shook.

"I'll go after her. I know where she'll be."

"Yes, please. Go. Quickly." Charlie's eyes flashed with agitation and his voice was low and urgent. "When you find her, will you do something for me? It's really important."

"Of course. Anything."

"Tell her I'll be waiting. I'll make my apologies to Henry and your mum. I'll go back to the shop. I'll leave the door unlocked. I'll be in the studio."

Charlie bent his head, but Nathan saw the tears in his eyes.

"God knows, I've waited fourteen years. I can wait another hour ... Please, Nathan, if you can. Bring her back to me."

14

The town, almost deserted, slept after Christmas lunch. Nathan could hear his own footsteps, see his breath chalk into the late afternoon air. A single figure on the beach ran with her dog. Low in the sky, a dying sun washed its face on the horizon, splashed the sea with pools of pink and gold.

The plateau stretched grey with pebbles, flattened with wild grass. Empty of Rosalie.

Panic clutched Nathan's heart.

*I was sure she'd be here.*

He scrambled up the rest of the cliff, stones flying, sand scratching his nails. He raced through the garden to the kitchen door.

*What if this time she's really run away?*

Tiggy ignored him, her shiny black haunches hunched over her dish.

*That's fresh food in Tiggy's bowl. Rosalie's been here. She'll be upstairs. Please let her be upstairs.*

But the attic stared blankly back.

Nathan cursed. A sharp, dark odour filled the air.

*That smells like sulphur. Someone's just lit a match. I know she's* been here. I can feel it in my bones. Now she's vanished again like she's flown away.

"Remember that night in the attic? She had candles. Maybe she's lit one of them."

But what for, Banksie? And where's she gone with it?

"There must be another way into the attic ... and out of it. A secret way."

Yes, of course. I never did find out where she'd vanished to that night.

"Well, maybe you can now. Try the walls. Run your fingers over them."

The walls by each of the windows stretched cool and solid beneath Nathan's hands. From the third wall, the stairs led down to the lower floor and the inside of the cottage. But along the fourth wall, where the art chest stood, a small cupboard squashed its triangular back into the corner.

Nathan remembered seeing it before, that afternoon when he and Rosalie had been packing. Then its doors were closed. Now they stood slightly ajar. Nathan opened them full out. A few old limply hanging jackets had been flung to one side. He pressed his hands against the wall behind them, felt the bump of a handle and pushed against it.

He gasped as a small opening gaped over a black hole.

*I've found something.*

He stooped, peered into the darkness.

*I can't really see, but I think it's a flight of iron steps. God knows where they lead ... I can't do anything without a light.*

"*Look around the attic. Those candles must be lying around somewhere. And matches.*"

Nathan scanned the shelves. Books, newspapers, boxes of chalks. On the desk a half-finished landscape. In the desk drawers ...

He pulled at the top drawer and saw a long, narrow box. He flicked it open and found four narrow candles, their wicks already burned. He scrabbled further and found a small box of matches.

He lit one of the candles and put another in his pocket, along with the matches. Then he turned towards the cupboard.

*I'm terrified. I don't know what I'm doing.*

"*Yes, you do. Looking for Rosalie.*"

Grimly, Nathan crawled down the iron steps. They spiralled steeply, cold beneath his right hand. His left held the candle, which sputtered into the gloom. At the bottom of the steps he stopped.

*I'm below ground level. I can't see much but I reckon there's a passageway that stretches ahead of me. The walls are slimy and freezing ... Everything smells sickly, a bit like beer, but it's stenchy and revolting.*

He shuddered.

*"Keep going, Weed. As fast as you can. If I'm right, the passage leads out to the sea."*

Nathan slithered on. The candle guttered and died. In the pitch darkness, he struggled with the matches, relit the smouldering wick and watched the shadows dance.

He heard the clink of bottles.

He stopped dead in his tracks, flattened himself against the passage wall. Its clammy coldness seeped into his back.

He felt moth-wings brush his face, once, twice, then over and over again, as if they were giving him some strange blessing. In the flickering darkness he heard a sharp, high call, like the shrieking of gulls, saying his name.

"Yes?" His terrified voice threw back its echo.

*"Keep her safe,"* the gulls seemed to shriek. *"Keep her very safe."*

"How can I?" Nathan shouted. The echo swirled into his ears. "I don't know where she is. I only wish I did."

His hand shook and the candle flickered wildly.

*"Find her ... and remember ... keep her safe."*

The echo died.

Shivering, Nathan pushed himself away from the wall and slithered down the passage.

A humming sound began its faint growling drawl.

It grew louder.

Nathan saw a chink of light.

It grew larger, wider.

He turned his body sideways, crushed it through a narrow crevice of rock.

And he was out of the passage, standing in rock pools thick with weed at the back of a cove, hearing the soft, rhythmic thunder of sea, the smell of salt and tar in his nostrils.

Rosalie stood near him, her back pressed against the cliff, her hands deep in her jacket pockets, her face wet with crying.

He said, "Thank God you're here."

She looked across at him. "So you've found me again. Right little sleuth, aren't you?"

Nathan gasped with relief at the salt air in his lungs. "I smelt sulphur in the attic. I worked it out from there. Was this where you went that night?"

"Where else?"

"The passageway's amazing. It must be hundreds of years old."

"They used to call our cottage Smuggler's Rest. You didn't know that, did you? My family ... Jake's parents and grandparents ... were smugglers all, so the story goes." She rubbed at her face with her sleeve. "It's in the blood, as they say. In the Croft veins and arteries." She gave her short, high laugh. "Not that *now* that's anything to do with me!"

"What do you mean? 'Course it's to do with you."

"No, it isn't. Not any more. Not after what Charlie's just told me."

"I don't understand –"

"It's simple enough, Nathan. My mother wasn't a Croft until she married my ... until she married Jake. And my *real* father isn't a Croft at all."

"Then who –?" Nathan gasped. "Are you saying – ?"

"Aren't I just? I'll give you three guesses, Nathan." Her voice was low, almost scathing. "Who's my real dad?"

"Is it Charlie?"

"Right first time! Isn't it simple when you know how?" She started to cry. "I've been completely and utterly betrayed. She never told me. Mum never told me. I thought I knew everything. That I could talk to her even though she's dead. I thought we were so close."

Nathan flailed, said stupidly, "Maybe she didn't know Charlie was – ?"

"Don't give me that." Angrily, she brushed at the tears. "Of course she knew. Remember those sketches, that painting?"

"Then she was protecting your ... keeping it from Jake. Keeping her marriage safe."

"Safe? How can you live in a pretend marriage when you know your child belongs to another man?"

"Perhaps she loved Jake too much to leave him?"

"Perhaps Jake knew about me ... about Charlie ... and *still* he wouldn't let Mum go." She stared out at the lift and swell of sea. "God, what a mess!"

He picked his way across the rock pools towards her. "I'm sorry. I wish your mum was still alive."

"It all makes sense now. How could I have been so dim? Mum and Charlie. It was always Mum and Charlie, all along. Who always bought her work for the shop? Who stuck by us so loyally when Dad – when *Jake* – was sent to prison?" Her eyes glimmered at him with their fierce blue light. "Who helped me that miserable afternoon when I was bunking off school?" Her voice dropped to a whisper. "Who's always treated me as if I were his daughter?"

"Charlie."

"Yes. Charlie. All the pieces fit together."

"But why did he never tell you?"

"He said Mum wouldn't let him. She made him promise he'd not tell me. She said maybe when I was sixteen, but not before. Charlie tried to keep his promise, although there were so many times after Mum died when he almost burst with wanting to. But finding out today about Dad's – about Jake's – accident was the last straw. He knew that if Jake had been killed, I'd have been totally on my own."

"So now –" Nathan hesitated, desperately wanting to bring a smile back to her tear-stained face. "Aren't you glad about all this? Being able to make sense of everything?"

"Part of me is." She shook her head. "But part of me still can't take it in, still doesn't understand. Can you imagine what it would be like if *you* found out your dad wasn't your dad?"

Nathan took her hand. "It seems to me," he said slowly, "there's only one thing you must do."

"What's that?"

"Talk to Charlie."

"I can't, Nathan. How can I face him?"

"He's waiting for you. He told me."

She snatched her hand away. "Where is he?"

"At the shop. In the studio. He said he'd waited fourteen

years for you and he could wait another hour. He begged me to bring you back."

"No." Blood seemed to drain from her face. "Oh, no. I can't deal with this."

She began to run across the beach to the rocks which heaved and pushed their way into the sea.

"Rosalie!" Nathan shouted. "Come back!"

The wind whipped his voice into a thin, useless cry.

He heard her call, "Leave me alone," as she stumbled over the sand, bent towards the rocks to clamber on to them, and then began to climb.

For a moment he stood paralysed. Then he began to follow, skidding on the edges of the rock pools, raising his head to check she was still there.

For an instant he saw her, outlined against the darkening sky, the wind raking back her hair, her pale face staring out at the sea. Then she seemed to slip. She threw out her arms to balance herself, fell backwards and tumbled over the rocks.

"Rosalie!"

Nathan felt the air rip from his lungs.

He lunged forwards across the sand, on to the rocks, to the point at which he'd seen her. He heard her voice shrieking for help.

He heard the cry of the gulls: *"Find her and keep her safe."* He looked down.

She was half in and half out of the sea, scrabbling at the teeth of the rocks, calling for him, trying to shake herself free of the waves, which returned over and again to smack against her face.

"Hold on!" He sat down on the rocks and began to slither his way towards her. "I'm here! I'm coming! Just hold on!"

Then something sharp ripped at his hands, made him cry out with pain. His right ankle wrenched at his body. He fell sideways, felt himself hurtling downwards, saw the foam on the waves rising towards him, crashed through their icy surface into the sea.

*I am in a pool, a vast swimming-pool, but it's colder than anything I have ever felt before. So cold that my mouth feels solid as ice.*

*Can't breathe. My ears are full of sound ... the sound of flooding ... and yet it's also deathly quiet as if everything is muffled. If I open my eyes, I can see rocks and pebbles and the bottom of the pool.*

*Except it's not the pool, it's the sea.*

*Of course, I have fallen into the sea.*

*I didn't mean to do this. The surface of the rocks was like a skating rink, the moss was green and slimy. Watch for the greenest bits, they're the worst. Treacherous.*

*Why am I wearing these clothes? They make everything so difficult. I can't move properly. I can taste salt. Bitter, it's so bitter. It's in my lungs and I can't cough it out.*

*Down, down ...*

*No —*

*No, help. Help me. Someone must help ...*

*But I'm on my own now, aren't I? No Dad. No Tom.*

*It's up to me. I must fight to come up.*

*Come on, fight ...*

*Swim upwards, up to the surface, up where there's more light, just a little more light, a rim of setting sun, red as blood on the water.*

*Go for the rim.*

*I can hear a voice. It's muffled, as if it's coming from another world.*

*It's calling my name.*

*I must push with my legs.*

*Harder.*

*A little more ...*

He crashed up through the waves into the air and gasped.

"Nathan!"

He saw the dark shape of somebody beside him, felt its heaviness.

Rosalie. She was here beside him.

He felt her arms lock around his shoulders. "Hold on to me. Don't let go ... Swim, Nathan, swim ... Don't go down again ... You mustn't go down."

Nathan coughed the water from his lungs and gasped again. "I won't." He shook the hair from his eyes. "Are you OK?"

"Yes. I slipped. I didn't mean to ... I was almost back on land when I looked up and saw you falling." He noticed how her mouth trembled, blue with cold. "I lost my grip again ... When I looked back at the sea, you'd vanished."

Her arms tightened around him. "Come on. Let's get out of this before we freeze to death."

They began to swim, more strongly now, back towards the shore. They clambered clumsily on to the edge of land. Like two soaked sea creatures, they lay panting for breath, the waves lapping at their ankles.

Nathan crawled to his feet, reached out his hands to Rosalie. Together, inch by inch, they slithered their way over the rocks, back to the cove. Water slurped and gurgled in his boots. Blood dripped from his grazed hands and his ankle ached.

Their arms around each other, they walked along the beach to the entrance to the passageway.

"God, Nathan." Rosalie stood looking at him. Her hair lay flat and wet, the colour of pale sand; water poured from her clothes. "For a moment there I thought you'd drowned."

"Thought I'd lost you too."

"I'm here."

"So am I."

In the relief and the laughter, slowly, awkwardly, Nathan took the girl in his arms. As they kissed he thought, *So this is what it's like.*

Minutes later, he heard a voice calling across the beach.

He opened his eyes.

The sky had slowly darkened around them.

"It's Charlie," he said. "He's found us."

15

"You're soaking wet, both of you!" Charlie scrambled across the beach towards them. "What's happened? Are you OK?"

"We slipped on the rocks." Nathan could still feel Rosalie's lips on his. He felt so strange: elated, freezing and yet pulsing with warmth. "She saved me."

"We saved each other," Rosalie said quietly. Her teeth started to chatter with cold.

Charlie moved towards her. "Have you told Nathan? ... About me?"

"Yes," Rosalie said. "I still can't take it in."

"You can't imagine how many times I've rehearsed telling you –"

"I'm scared, Charlie –"

"Don't be. That's the last thing I want."

"So what *do* you want?"

"Right now? To take you home ... take you *both* home ... Get you warm and dry."

"And then?"

"Hear me out. That's all I ask. Give me a chance. Let me

tell you what happened. Then you can decide what to do." The last streaks of light shone in his eyes. "If you never want to see me again, I'll understand."

Nathan felt Rosalie leave the shelter of his arm. She moved over to Charlie and took his hand.

"It's a deal," she said.

Charlie had pushed them into his car, driven fast through the deserted streets. "Rosalie, put on some dry clothes at the flat and come straight round to the studio. Nathan, I'll find you some jeans and a sweater. They'll be a bit big, but a sight better than sitting in seaweed!"

Now, huddled in Charlie's clothes, clutching a mug of steaming tea beside the fire in the studio, plasters on his grazed hands, his ankle swollen and sore, Nathan could smell salt on his skin. Every so often his body shivered with cold and fear as he remembered those moments in the sea, then trembled with excitement as he remembered that first kiss.

The studio was a wide, friendly room, its white walls hung with Charlie's cartoons, its desk littered with papers and pens. Nathan gazed around it, reassured and comforted, watching Rosalie's face as she sat beside Charlie, noticing for the first time how alike father and daughter looked.

"Tell me the whole story," Rosalie said. "There's so much I want to know."

"When Jake Croft and I were young," Charlie said, "we were best friends. Then it became something fiercer. We started to compete. Best marks in maths, most goals in football. We were all at school together. Moira was two years younger. She and I met properly at a school dance and I couldn't take my eyes off her. We talked and danced all evening. Then I walked her home ... I've loved her ever since.

"Jake was jealous as hell. He asked Moira out just to compete with me. That's how it started. Then he became obsessed with her. Wouldn't leave her alone, followed her everywhere, took her out whenever she'd agree to go.

"Moira knew I wanted to marry her, but I had to get a decent training. As an artist I had nothing to offer her. No money, nothing. I had to make it on my own. So I went to an art college in London. For a year we survived more or less, just by writing to each other. I came down here for long weekends, she came to see me in the Smoke.

"Until one morning I got a letter telling me she'd married Jake. He'd inherited the boat yard and the cottage.

Everything he needed had fallen into his lap. Moira wanted to paint, it was all she'd ever wanted. She said she was fond of Jake, that she thought he'd look after her.

"I was beside myself. She'd given me no warning, not a word. I swore I'd never see her again, that I'd go abroad. France, Spain, anywhere. But when it came to the crunch, I didn't. I got a job in London while I was still at college, drawing cartoons for a local newspaper. I made contacts, useful ones. Somebody offered me a job as a cartoonist on a new magazine. A once-in-a-lifetime opportunity. I took it. I needed the money, to be kept occupied.

"I took other girls out in London. I had other lovers. But every morning, all I could hear was Moira's voice, all I could see was her face, in the mirror, in the sky. I simply couldn't forget her."

"So you came home?"

"My father died. I came back for the funeral. I tried to keep away from Moira but I couldn't help myself. I called on her at the cottage." He smiled at Rosalie. "She almost fainted at the sight of me. We walked down the garden, on to the plateau. It was the most marvellous morning, the first spring day of the year. The sea was so calm and quiet, the beach seemed to be waiting for us. It was as if our London years apart had never happened.

"Moira told me things with Jake were tough. He was working all hours at the boat yard, expanding the business, going to France to chase new contacts. She was often alone, more often than she could bear. And there was something else, although she never actually said."

"What, Charlie?"

"She was always afraid of Jake. Frightened of what he might do to her if she told him the truth ... She still loved me. She made that absolutely clear. She regretted marrying Jake, but she was going to stay loyal to him through thick and thin.

"I knew I'd have to come back to St Ives, whether Moira left Jake or not. I had to be near her, see her whenever I could. We said it all that morning on the plateau. When Henry gave me the job as cartoonist on the *St Ives Recorder* I was overjoyed. I rented a cottage at Carnstabba, behind Tregenna, saved every penny I could to buy this place. Moira and I spoke to each other on the phone every day, met whenever we could. It was much more than an affair. In our hearts, we were married, constant companions, best friends.

"Ten years went by. Moira wanted a baby, but she'd given up all hope of having one. When she finally told me she was pregnant, we both knew you were our child."

Rosalie said slowly, "I've got to ask you this, Charlie. When Mum died that morning in June, she was on the plateau ... But she didn't have her sketchbook or anything. I always thought she must've been going to meet someone." Her face was pale. "Was it you?"

Charlie leaned forward in his chair and took her hands. "Yes."

Rosalie's eyes were bright with tears. "What happened?"

"Moira and Jake had had a row the night before. A friend of Jake's in the pub had told Jake he'd seen me and Moira together. Jake was sick with jealousy. He started shouting at Moira, told her she must never see me again. The next morning he left for France on one of his wild-goose chases to get a new job.

"Moira rang me. She started to cry. She said she was scared Jake would get violent and that we had to stop seeing each other. I wouldn't hear of it. I wanted her to leave Jake, make a clean breast of everything, tell him you were my daughter. Moira said no, it would destroy him, she had to see me, maybe for the last time.

"I shut the shop and waited for her here. She never arrived and I went crazy. I ran down to the beach, but by the time I got there, the ambulance crew had taken her away."

Charlie buried his face in his hands.

"When I was waiting for you this afternoon, I thought – God, don't let this happen to me again. I can't lose Rosalie as well." He raised his head. "You can't know how much I loved her ... How much she loved me."

"I *do* know." Rosalie knelt beside him. "Nathan and I were clearing the attic. We found lots of sketches Mum did of you ... and a painting, a beautiful oil."

"What happened to them?"

"Dad ... Jake destroyed them. I wanted to give you the painting. But the moment he saw it he went mad." She bent her head. "It's so hard now. Moving out of the attic, having so little left of her work. That's the hardest thing of all ... There's so little of her left."

Charlie reached out to touch her hair. "There's more than you think."

"What do you mean?" She was startled. "How can there be?"

He stood up, held out his hand. "Come and see. I can show you now. Both of you."

They followed him out of the room, up a narrow flight of stairs. Three doors led off from the landing.

"That's my kitchen," said Charlie, "that's my bathroom, that's my bedroom. Boring and ordinary." He gestured to a second flight of stairs. "But up there, in the attic, that's different. Up there, I have a surprise for you."

Charlie switched on the lights, which fanned against three walls. From the fourth, a long, curtainless window revealed the inky blue sky, lit with stars, the waterfront, lights from the boats bobbing in the sea.

The smell of paint and polish hung in the air. On the floor, Nathan felt soft pale carpet brush beneath his bare feet. In a corner, a low couch boasted immaculate cushions.

And above the wall lights, below them and beside them hung paintings of every shape and size – oils and watercolours – charcoal and pencil sketches, photographs, reviews, each precisely framed and labelled.

Nathan knew without being told what he was looking at.

Rosalie stood in the centre of the room as if she were frozen, her hands on her mouth.

Charlie flung an arm around her shoulders. "All your mum's work," he said. "I bought everything I could, whenever I could, supported her through thick and thin, looked at her paintings and sketches, watched her while she worked, commented, helped her in every which way.

She was a great artist, Rosalie. And you're going to follow in her footsteps."

Rosalie began to sob. She turned towards Charlie.

"Don't cry, little one. We'll always be able to remember her with these."

Rosalie raised her head, stared across the room. "Those are the landscapes we asked you to sell for us when Jake went to prison." She moved towards them, ran her fingers over the thick oils.

"Yes," Charlie said proudly. "Aren't they wonderful?" He pointed to another wall. "And what do you think of that?"

"My *Figures on a Beach.* You've got that too."

Nathan moved closer to look at it. Moira and Charlie, pushing together across a stormy beach.

"It was as if you'd given me a key," Charlie said. "To unlock everything. Your own marvellous new work."

Rosalie moved over to the window. She looked out over the waterfront, at the sky spattered with stars. "Thank you, Charlie."

"What for?"

"For this ... all this. For loving Mum as you did. For having me."

"Good God, child. What are you thanking me for?" He stood behind her, his hands on her shoulders. "You and

Moira. You're what my entire life has been about."

"Come to think of it," Rosalie turned. Her eyes had captured the starlight. "Maybe it's Nathan I should thank, for bringing us together."

He stood at the top of the cul-de-sac.

Boxing Day. An hour to go before he and Mum left for London, their bags packed; Mum talking to Grandpa at Tregenna about lawyers and surveyors and all the details of buying; about finding a new school they could see at half-term.

Rosalie had rung him from the flat, asked whether he had time to meet her at the cottage. She said she had something important to ask him, and something to give him, but refused to tell him any more.

He walked towards the cottage. The sore ankle made it hard to run, but his hands were healing fast.

*This is going to be my home. I can still hardly believe it. I was in such a state yesterday, trying to find Rosalie, I hardly noticed the place, only that I'd have dug through a mountain to find her.*

He tapped on the kitchen door, creaked it open and grinned.

Rosalie, washing dishes in the sink, looked up. "I meant to say thank you for yesterday. So rude of me, rushing off like that, after such a lunch. Your mum and grandpa must have thought I was crazy."

"That you'd found your real dad? Not bad for a Christmas afternoon!"

Tiggy purred up at him, twisted around his legs. "Hello, cat."

Rosalie dried her hands. "That's what I wanted to give you. Tiggy's yours if you'd like her."

Nathan gasped. "I'd *love* her ... Do you mean –?"

"Could we leave her here? Martha can feed her until you move in, I'll be calling in to keep her company. If I take her to the fish-and-chip-shop flat, she'll never stay. She'll run back to her patch, this cottage, this garden. Specially the garden – it belongs to her ... Doesn't it, Tig? This is your special home, like it was mine."

Nathan bent, took Tiggy in his arms, buried his face in the warmth of glossy fur. He remembered that afternoon when her yellow eyes had first inspected him, welcomed him, above the grey stone pond.

"I've never had a cat before. I'd love to take care of Tiggy." They perched on a stool together. "But she'll always belong to you. We will share her, won't we?"

She looked at them both. "We will."

Tiggy slithered from his arms, leaving a cool, lonely

space on his shoulder.

"So you've gone back to Jake's flat? You won't be living with Charlie?"

"I can't just abandon Jake, can I? Especially not now, not with all his good resolutions. He's always been Dad to me, looked after me for fourteen years. He's done his best to love me. I know he adored Mum, would never have harmed a hair of her head. If he can really lay off the booze, I reckon we're going to get through all this together."

"So he doesn't know you've found out about Charlie?"

"No. I couldn't tell him. He looks so frail and tired. It would kill him."

"And what about Charlie's attic?"

"I'll see a lot of Charlie. He says I can work in his studio. He's going to buy me a desk. I've told him about Dad's drinking ... he knew about it anyway, but now if things get bad again I've got someone to turn to. But his attic –"

"Yes?"

"It's Mum's room, isn't it? Charlie's and Moira's. It's not meant for me."

She turned from the table, held out her hand. "Though I want to put something in it. Hang a new painting on the wall. If you've got the time. If you don't mind."

His fingers touched hers, cool and damp. "Mind what?"

"I need a new sketch."

"You mean – ?"

"Of someone called Nathan Fielding."

He laughed. "You want to draw me?"

"Yes. Give me half an hour. Sit in the attic. In one of those scruffy armchairs."

"It'll cost you ..."

"Oh? How much?"

"A thousand kisses." He blushed at her smile, took her awkwardly in his arms. "Three now. *Many* more later."

They climbed the stairs into the attic. In spite of the sunlight, Nathan shivered.

Rosalie looked at him. "What's wrong?"

"Nothing," Nathan said. He stared at the centre of the room. "It's just that –"

"You're remembering the ghosts."

"How did you know?"

"It'll be easier now ... Their spirits will be still. Now I've found Charlie and I can look at Mum's work whenever I need to."

He gave a sigh of relief. "I thought perhaps the ghosts were warning me off."

"No." She looked at him, her eyes warm, approving. "They'd never have let you see them if they didn't want you here."

She pulled out a sketchbook from a huddle on the desk, busied with charcoal pieces.

"Sit over there."

He slumped into an armchair.

"Turn sideways ... Drop your head a bit ... Relax ... Perfect." She reached for a book. "Here. Read this while I draw."

Nathan looked at the cover. "Hey," he said. "*Lord of the Flies*. How did you know? I've been meaning to read this for ages."

"Sure you have." She settled the sketchbook on her knees. "I can read your mind, Nathan Fielding, so you'd better watch what you're thinking!"

He grinned.

He looked at the graceful slope of her shoulder, the way her hair fell half across her face, her forehead puckered in concentration, her hand as it moved swiftly over the smoothness of paper.

"Girl in the attic," he murmured.

She glanced up at him, her eyes bright, teasing. "Boy in the garden?"

"You remember that day I first saw you?"

"Of course."

"Remember what you said? About my being too late to do anything?"

"'Course I remember."

"You were wrong. Admit it ... I wasn't too late, was I?"

In the silence he heard the pounding of his heart; the scrape of her charcoal; gulls calling to each other over the sea.

"No," Rosalie said. She smiled at him. "No, you were just in time."

Valerie Mendes was born in Buckinghamshire and went to North London Collegiate School. Soon after taking a double honours degree in English and Philosophy at Reading University, she moved to Oxford, where she still lives. She is, proudly, the mother of the theatre and film director, Sam Mendes CBE.

Valerie started writing stories when she was six. That summer she spent the first of many holidays in St Ives, Cornwall – a place which for her has always been particularly special, and where most of this story is set.

*Girl in the Attic* is her ninth published book and first full-length novel.

# The Raging Quiet

*The Raging Quiet* is a haunting and compelling story about the power and determination to overcome prejudice and injustice in a world of witchcraft, feudalism and intolerance.

Set in Medieval times, it tells the story of Marnie and Raver each set apart from the community around them: Marnie because she is a newcomer having been brought to the seaside village by her new - and much older - husband; and Raver because he is the village lunatic.

*The Raging Quiet* - though embedded in a historical setting - has undiminished relevance today; Marnie and Raver are singled out because they are different.

ISBN 0 689  82706 7

# Young Nick's Head

THE YEAR IS 1768, Nicholas Young's mind is made up. He's had enough! Enough of the cruel butcher to whom he is apprenticed and enough of his indifferent father lurking somewhere in the background of his existence. He's had enough of the squalor of his life in London. He is going to run away.

But when he's stowed away on board a small ship he has no idea how famous this journey will be, one of the most famous journeys of discovery in maritime history. Three years it will take before he'll come back to London, three long years of adventure and hardship: an eleven-year-old boy among eighty tough-minded, seafaring men and under constant scrutiny from the gentlemen on board. There's midshipman Bootie who makes every day a living hell for Nick and John Ravenhill the drunken sail maker. But Dr Monkhouse, the surgeon, and Mr Banks, the botanist, stand up for their keen and gifted assistant and one by one Nick befriends the crew.

ISBN 0 689 83508 6

# Raspberries on the Yangtze

The Yangtze in this story is not China's biggest waterway, but a rather magical place on the outskirts of a small town in the backwoods of Quebec, Canada.

Nancy, who tells the story, is down-to-earth, practical and dead keen to know everything. Her main challenge in life is her elder brother Andrew. Nancy calls him a 'big thinker'. Their mother calls Andrew a 'dreamer'.

With a few quick brush strokes Karen Wallace transports the reader to a time and a place where children enjoyed a freedom that is impossible to imagine today. The plot moves along quickly, its profound observations and simple truths skilfully unveiled through vivid and authentic dialogue. It's the story of a summer when old dreams are shattered and new dreams are born. For Nancy and her friends, things will never be the same.

ISBN 0 689 82796 2

# For Maritsa, With Love

Young Maritsa ignores the angry voices, the insults and the threats. She's heard it all before, and worse. Begging is what she does, and she's good at her job. She knows just how to appeal to the rich commuters of the Paris Metro, how to soften their hearts with her forlorn face and her crumpled tragic note. But somehow, Maritsa knows it's not forever. She catches a glance of a different world and starts dreaming of a career in the movies: pretty dresses and trinkets, fine  house and parties…

Turning her back on the gypsy family she lives with and striking out on her own, Maritsa meets that man in the  dark glasses and his pretty wife again. They've promised her a screen test. Maritsa will go home famous – at least, that's what she thinks. But soon young, vulnerable Maritsa is being drawn into a dark and seedy underworld, to somewhere nobody should ever have to go.

ISBN 0 689  83636 8